SECRET REFUGE

DANA MENTINK

D0029275

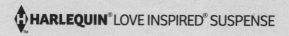

HARLEQUIN® LOVE INSPIRED® SUSPENSE

Recycling programs
for this product may
not exist in your area.

™ LOVE INSPIRED BOOKS

ISBN-13: 978-0-373-67672-9

Secret Refuge

www.Harlequin.com

Printed in U.S.A.

If thou, Lord, shouldest mark iniquities,
O Lord, who shall stand?
—Psalms 130:3

For those special needs children
who have flown into my life and taught me about love.

"I thought you left town."

"Came back." Mick's gaze made Keeley squirm.

"What do you want?" Keeley asked.

"Do you have reason to think Tucker knows the child is his?"

"What are you talking about?"

"The little girl your sister gave birth to. Tucker's the father, isn't he?"

"Who do you think you are?" she said, fear sparking into anger. "Coming into my life and prying into private information that you have no right to. June is mine, I'm her legal guardian, and her biological father is none of your business."

"It's Tucker's business. He's come back to take her and punish you."

"You have no right to interfere. You're not a cop."

"I'm trying to help."

"The time to help was when Tucker should have been under house arrest. You helped then, didn't you? You made sure he was a free man, and then he killed my sister."

"I...don't want to cause you any more pain."

"Then go away."

Dana Mentink is an award-winning author of Christian fiction. Her novel *Betrayal in the Badlands* won a 2010 RT Reviewers' Choice Award, and she was pleased to win the 2013 Carol Award for *Lost Legacy*. She has authored more than a dozen Love Inspired Suspense novels. Dana loves feedback from her readers. Contact her via her website at danamentink.com.

Books by Dana Mentink

Love Inspired Suspense

Wings of Danger Series

Hazardous Homecoming
Secret Refuge

Stormswept Series

Shock Wave
Force of Nature
Flood Zone

Treasure Seekers Series

Lost Legacy
Dangerous Melody
Final Resort

Visit the Author Profile page at Harlequin.com for more titles

ONE

The handprint showed clearly in the dust on her driver's-side window, as if someone had leaned there to look inside Keeley Stevens's Jeep.

Who would be looking inside her aged vehicle? Nothing worth stealing in there.

The outline on the glass blurred as she washed the imprint away with the hose.

His face, Tucker's face, rose from the shadows of memory. Her sister's murderer. He had long fingers like that.

"Knock it off, Keeley," she told herself. It was purely melodrama. She never should have watched that black-and-white mystery movie marathon the night before. The handprint was the work of a teen messing around, no doubt the kids she'd hassled earlier in the week. Or maybe her paranoia had taken root the morning before, when she'd noticed the long-haired man watching her from across the street as she gassed up her car. He was too far away to see clearly. Just a guy enjoying a smoke. Normal.

She would not let a teen prank and her own nerves undo her. And no more mystery marathons. Strictly the cooking channel. Maybe she'd learn how to make something with more than three ingredients.

When the rinsing was complete, she loaded up her Jeep and drove out of town, heater turned on to high to fend off the early-spring chill. It had to be the cold that made her skin prickle, because she would not allow fear to nest in her soul. Once she did, it would lay down roots and conquer her. Keeley would not be conquered. Ever. But still the feeling that started when she saw the long-haired man remained alive in her stomach, somewhere down deep.

Had Tucker returned?

I murdered your sister, and now it's your turn, she imagined him saying.

"Toughen up, girl," she muttered to herself. Tucker was no doubt hiding from the cops in some faraway city. He'd murdered LeeAnn nearly two years ago, only two months after his parole agent had allowed for the removal of his tracking bracelet. Ironic, since he'd never been incarcerated for anything other than car theft, not a violent offender. No, not violent, until the day he'd smashed in Lee-Ann's skull and stuffed her body into the trunk of his car, intending to flee.

And if he had made a successful escape? Would she ever have known what had happened to her sister? But LeeAnn had been able to send one frantic text before he killed her.

Tucker. Help me.

Keeley recalled the icy fear that had gripped her body as she'd dialed the police that day. They hadn't been able to save LeeAnn. Tucker had crashed the car into a pond, escaped custody and gone on the run.

Nowhere near.

Tucker was just a bad memory, but what if she did come face-to-face with him one day?

Keeley ground her teeth. He would be the one to lose.

No good news ever came at three o'clock in the morning. Mick Hudson knew that from his days as a marine in Iraq and his years as a parole officer in Portland. He cracked an eye open, rolled over and snatched up the old phone on the second ring before it could wake his father.

"Mick?" the voice said.

"Who wants to know?" His usual hospitable greeting. Whoever had broken the still of the small house tucked deep in the secluded bird sanctuary in the Oregon mountains did not deserve courtesy. Yet.

"It's Reggie." A dry chuckle. "You've been in the woods so long you can't recognize a civilized voice? Retirement hasn't mellowed you."

Mick sat up. Reggie Donaldson had been his

supervisor when he was a parole officer, before the murder had torn his life apart. "What's going on?"

Reggie sighed. "Ever the one for charming small talk."

"You want small talk, you don't call at three in the morning."

There was a long pause. Mick braced himself for the news. Whatever it was, it was going to hurt. "My sources say Tucker Rivendale's been spotted in Oregon."

Mick's heart jumped up into a higher gear. "When?"

"Yesterday. I made some calls and the cops are on it, but so far no arrest. Small town. They don't have the resources. They said they would contact you for info, but I knew you'd rather hear it from me."

"Where you figure he was heading?"

Another long pause. "I could be wrong."

"You usually aren't. Where?"

Reggie blew out a breath. "If I had to guess, I'd say he's on his way to Keeley Stevens's place in Silver Creek."

A slow roar started up in Mick's ears. Tucker Rivendale was the one he'd misjudged, the man he'd vouched for who'd murdered Keeley's sister, LeeAnn. Mick's error had cost LeeAnn her life. He flashed for a moment on her wide grin, the way she would greet everyone from postal worker to parole officer with a hug. With her arm around Tucker, they were an adoring couple, or so he'd thought, right up until the moment he'd learned that Tucker had killed her.

"Mick? You still there?"

He forced the answer past dry lips. "Yeah."

"Just thought you'd want to know. I knew you were going to catch wind of it, so better to hear it from me."

Oh, yeah. He wanted to know, all right.

"You're not going to do anything risky, are you? I'm headed up there, and it's better for you to stay away," Reggie said, betraying the smallest hint of excitement in his voice.

"You still need to follow the rules if you want to keep your job."

Reggie laughed. "Since when did I ever worry about the rules?"

"I'll handle it."

Reggie paused and Mick could hear the smile. "Cops won't want you interfering. I'll call and see if I can grease the wheels for you. Try not to get killed, huh?"

"Yes, sir." Mick disconnected. He stood, letting the Oregon spring chill his skin and assimilate with the cold that had settled there permanently when he'd let Tucker Rivendale murder Keeley's sister.

Keeley pushed the old Jeep a little faster, and the engine complained as it took the mountain slope just before dusk. The morning shoot had gone flawlessly, and her courage was on the mend. Keeley Stevens, world-class avian photographer, at her finest. Now it was time for the night shots of the great horned owl emerging from the nest. One good picture of the powerful, yellow-eyed predator would net her three hundred dollars, which meant gas in the car, food on the table and utilities paid for another month anyway.

She squeezed the steering wheel as the engine's growling grew louder. Her sister would have given the vehicle a pep talk about little train engines and such. Keeley took a different tact. "If you leave me stranded on this road and I miss my shot, I'm turning you in for scrap. You'll be a toaster by morning."

Big words. She hardly had the money to replace her crippled toaster, let alone a new vehicle. As it was, she was still driving LeeAnn's beat-up Jeep, picturing her sister clutching the armrest, urging Keeley to slow down.

I'm not in a hurry to leave this world, sis.

Ah, but you did leave it, Lee. And God took you way too early. Her throat thickened. What she wouldn't give to hear her little sister's gentle criticisms one more time. *You were always too sweet, Lee.*

Too trusting, right up until she was murdered just before her twenty-sixth birthday. Too innocent to see it coming. Naive about a man who said he loved her. Not a mistake Keeley was going to make.

Cold air whooshed in through the open driver's-side window along with crisp scent of pine and fir. She thought she heard the whine of a motorbike. Ahead? Behind? She stopped to listen. Nothing. Was it the tiny flicker of a headlamp she'd seen flitting through the dark tree trunks? No, nothing but that paranoia. LeeAnn's murder had stripped away her naive sense of safety, depositing a shadow just behind her shoulder that taunted her vision as much as she wanted to deny it, kept her from letting people close. *See what can happen?* it whispered. *Remember how easily your sister's life was extinguished?* She swallowed.

"Get the shot and leave your paranoia at home," she muttered to herself. She took the steep turn slowly, no sense making too much noise. As it was, her quarry was extremely sensitive to the slightest vibration, so she'd have to park soon and hike up the mountain on foot.

Her Nikon camera and tripod with the gimbal head rested safely on the passenger seat. They were her most precious belongings. Well, second most anyway. She got that strange, fuzzy feeling deep down in her gut, along with a swirl of desperation. She could not give up, in spite of the ever-present fatigue. Her life wasn't just about herself anymore. She had someone else relying on her, someone with flyaway hair that never stayed in pigtails and a ready smile.

Something cracked into the windshield, and her

foot reflexively hit the brake. She stopped, engine idling. The wheels must have kicked up a rock. She probably had a new chip in the front windshield to show for it. She started on more slowly when another pebble hit the front glass. This time she put the Jeep in Park, slamming the door open.

"All right, Ricky and Stephano. Knock it off," she hissed to the teen boys she knew must be hunkered down behind the boulders off the path. "If you scare my owl away, I'll have you tossed in jail." She was on shaky ground here and the boys probably knew it. She'd threatened to cause trouble with their parents when they vandalized her shed, but incarceration for rock throwing might be a tad severe. Ricky and Stephano were rabble-rousers, but probably not ready for prison yet. In any case, they might just mess up her opportunity to photograph the bird she'd been stalking for a month.

There was a crackle of dry leaves, and someone stepped from behind the rocks. Baggy pants, dirty sweatshirt, backpack. She could not see his face in the near darkness, just a white gleam as he turned his face to hers. Long hair.

Something in the body language made her skin erupt in prickles. Was it the slope of the shoulders, the way he tucked a thumb into the belt loop of his jeans? She knew it was Tucker, even before he spoke. All the time she'd been hunting the owl, he'd been hunting her. Tingles of fear coursed along and tangled with white-hot rage.

"So," she said, forcing the words out around the serrated edge in her throat. "Are you here to kill me now, too?"

He didn't answer, just stared at her with eyes that gleamed reptilian in the dim light.

She took a small step back toward the open car door. The motion seemed to jar him loose from his thoughts.

He moved fast, coming at her straight on. She had just enough time to get into the car and slam the door, jamming the lock down. His eyes went wide as he tried the handle, banging his palms against the glass. She started the engine and he backed off. Lurching forward, she lost sight of him and then she realized her mistake. She had not locked the passenger-side door.

Tucker's face loomed in the darkness, fingers yanking at the handle. Though she jammed the accelerator down, the wheels found no traction on the muddy ground, spinning grit and squealing their helplessness. She tried Reverse with no better luck. Tucker dived into the seat, hands grabbing at her forearms. With a scream, she threw an elbow as hard as she was able into his face and felt the give of his cheek. Momentarily, he released his grip, grunting in pain.

She pressed the gas again and the car shot forward, tumbling him to the floor. He tried to right himself, and she took her foot off the gas pedal long enough to kick out at him. He shoved her off.

"I want what's mine…" he began, and then suddenly he was pulled from the car. A tall stranger with a crew cut had Tucker by the shoulders. He looked vaguely familiar. Tucker whipped around and threw a punch, which glanced off the stranger's chin, sending him slightly off balance, but he straightened quickly. Through the open door, over the sound of her own shuddering breaths, she heard the guy say, "You're done, kid."

Then there was a glint of metal, a shine of a blade in Tucker's hands. A knife.

"I'll die first, Mick," he hissed. "I've got nothing more to lose."

Keeley realized she'd taken her foot off the gas. Now, with a flood of crazy energy, she cranked the car forward then into a tight turn and stepped on the accelerator. The open door bumped and banged, but she did not take a moment to close it. Both men jerked their heads in her direction.

Tucker yelled something. She did not stop.

The car zipped forward, pinging gravel and dirt up. She was gratified to see the men scatter, running. Her front wheel hit a depression, causing the wheels to buck, and she fought to stay the course.

He would not win. Not again.

Mick saw the blur of the moving vehicle bearing down on him. The shock loosened his grip, and Tucker slashed with the knife, cutting into Mick's biceps. Fire rippled through his arm. Then the Jeep was upon them. Tucker leaped aside. With no time to do the same, Mick dived for the trees.

Too slow.

For a moment, he was airborne, cartwheeling over the hood of the car and tumbling headfirst onto the hard ground. The breath rushed out of him in a painful explosion. He tried to get to his feet, stumbled and fell, finding himself planted palms first in the dirt.

Where was Tucker? His nerves screamed. He looked up in time to see the flash of a T-shirt as the kid took off for the trees. Forcing his legs into motion, he made it to his feet.

Keeley got out of the car. She was slender, her hair chin length, cut in a careless bob showing under the knit cap. The same blue eyes as her sister. She looked older and more tired than he'd seen her the last time at LeeAnn's funeral, the lines more pronounced around her mouth. At least, he thought they were more pronounced. Blink as he would, her face blurred in his vision. He heard her speak as if from far away.

"Who are you?" she said.

I'm the man who let Tucker Rivendale kill your sister, his mind said.

She hugged herself, waiting for him to respond.

Mick struggled to speak. *Get back in the car and drive before he comes back. Don't let him hurt you like he did LeeAnn.* But his mouth remained stubbornly closed. "I think I know you. Tell me who you are," she demanded again.

"Mick," he said aloud, or maybe it was only in his mind as his sight bled off into darkness and his knees buckled under him.

TWO

Spider.

He swam back into consciousness, staring up at a ceiling upon which sat a fat black spider, motionless on the cracked plaster. Then he was assaulted by memories of Tucker and his own body impacting the front of a Jeep. A vulnerable woman's face, eyes round with shock, materialized in his memory. Keeley. He jerked upright, head spinning, sliding a little on the sheet draped over the couch.

Keeley stood, motion arrested midstride, in the middle of the room, a roll of gauze in one hand and a phone in the other.

"The police are on their way," she said. "Ambulance, too."

He planted both feet on the floor, willing it to stop moving. "Don't need an ambulance. Are you okay?"

She nodded. "I was the one driving, remember? You're the guy who got run over."

He felt his lips curling into a painful grin against

the scratches on his face. "Yeah. Why did you do that anyway? Women usually need to get to know me better before they want to run me over."

She shrugged, unsmiling. "Adrenaline." She set the gauze on the fruit crate that served as a coffee table. "Your arm is bleeding. Sorry to ask, but could you try not to drip on the couch? It's third-hand, but it's the nicest piece of furniture I own."

He dutifully wrapped his wound as best he could. She did not offer to help, and that was just fine with Mick. His stomach knotted now that he was here in the same room with her, the woman who had circled the edges of his mind for almost two years. The place smelled of toasted bread. Warm, cozy, worn furniture and a bookshelf crammed with photography magazines and old VHS tapes. On the tiny kitchen table was a stack of multihued paper and three pairs of scissors in varying sizes.

"I remember who you are," she said softly. "I looked through your wallet. You're Mick Hudson. Tucker Rivendale's parole officer."

He swallowed. "I was, yes. I don't do that job anymore." He felt the pain of a deeper injury throbbing. And what should he say now? "I'm sorry" seemed a little thin. "I made a terrible mistake" came off even weaker.

"You met with my sister often."

Each word cut a fresh wound. "Yes. When she and Tucker began dating again, I got to know her on some of my visits. She…she was a great lady."

Great lady. Was that all he could offer?

"Yes." She stared at him and the moment stretched long and taut, like the anchor line holding tight to a storm-tossed boat.

A slight smile quirked her lips. "I thought you would be uglier when I first met you at LeeAnn's that one time."

He blinked. "What?"

"LeeAnn only spoke of Mick the parole officer. I pictured you as a gorilla type, with a broken nose and slicked-back hair. And younger. I thought you'd be younger than you turned out to be."

He shifted. He'd only seen Keeley a handful of times when he supervised Tucker, and usually it was only for a brief moment. "I suppose the ugly part is relative, but I'm forty." Forty going on ancient. He searched her face, unable to read below the calm that he imagined was a front. She was thirty-four, he knew, like he also knew where she and her sister had been born. And that they had a mother living in a retirement home in Colorado and a father deceased, thanks to the ravages of lung cancer when the girls were young. A head full of information that lingered along with the memories.

"I…" He cleared his throat. "Did you see which direction Tucker went?" Lame, but at least it filled up the silence.

"No. I stopped paying attention when I lugged you into the Jeep and brought you here."

He started to say something, some rough thank-you or another, but she cut him off. A good thing. Saved him from saying something stupid.

"You probably have a concussion. Should see to that, and maybe you need stitches." She pointed. "Your bandage is oozing."

He swathed himself in more gauze, mindful of the couch.

The sounds of sirens drifted through the night. A fist pounded on the door and Keeley jumped, fear crowding her fine cerulean eyes.

Too soon for cops. He put a finger to his lips and went to the window, moving the curtain slightly. Guy on the porch wasn't Tucker. A tall, lean man dressed in running gear, sweat-damp hair curling around his ears.

"Keeley? It's John." More pounding. "Open the door."

Keeley sighed and, against Mick's better judgment, she unlocked the bolt and let John in, leaving the door ajar.

John enveloped her in a strong embrace, Keeley's chin barely reaching his shoulder. "Are you all right? I just got back from my run and turned on the police radio channel. You called in. An attacker?" His eyes shifted suddenly as he caught sight of Mick. He pushed her away and tensed, fists ready. "Who are you?"

Mick sighed, holding up his palms. "Mick Hudson. I was trying to assist Keeley when she was attacked. Rivendale got away, but he's probably not far."

"Rivendale?" John's eyes narrowed, face gone pale. "I never thought he'd come back. He's a nervy psycho, isn't he?"

In Mick's experience most psychos had plenty of nerve, and they looked exactly like normal people.

"And you are?"

"John Bender."

The sirens were deafening now as the police pulled up to the house.

John moved toward the door.

"Stay still," Mick said. "Cops are tense when they respond code three. Don't give them more reason to be nervous."

John shot him a look filled with venom. "I don't think you can count yourself as a law enforcement expert anymore, can you, Mr. Hudson? Didn't you leave that arena after you let Rivendale loose to murder Keeley's sister? I know all about it."

Mick's first reaction was to get in the guy's face, but the wave of guilt that followed kept him silent.

"That was the worst moment of my life." John continued to stare at him. "I loved LeeAnn. If things had turned out different, she would have been my wife."

Mick was surprised. Being Tucker Rivendale's parole officer, he'd known that Tucker loved LeeAnn and she returned the feeling. As far as he knew, they'd been exclusive since LeeAnn returned to Silver Creek. Never had he even heard John Bender's name mentioned. He shot a look at Keeley, but she didn't meet his eye.

He'd missed something. Again.

You didn't know a lot of things, Mick. If you had, LeeAnn wouldn't be dead.

In the following hour, three cops handled the investigation, interviewing them. Keeley sat calmly on the still-clean sofa, John holding her hand.

Something about the gangly man annoyed Mick, but then, holing up on his family's raptor sanctuary since he quit his job hadn't given him a lot of practice getting along with people. John Bender, as Mick soon figured out, was an avian veterinarian. LeeAnn had worked as his part-time receptionist. Mick remembered LeeAnn mentioned something about studying to become a vet someday.

Mick sat quietly, listening to every detail until the chief, a short, stocky man by the name of Uttley, finished up.

"Roadblocks are set up and we've got people coming from the area response team to help with a door-to-door search."

"He can easily stay in the woods," Mick said.

The chief raised an eyebrow and patted his front pocket until he found a butterscotch candy, which he stuck in his cheek. "How you figure?"

"He was a big camper back in the day. Almost an

Eagle Scout before he started getting into trouble. Loved the survivalist stuff."

The chief sucked, mouth working as he took in Mick's information. "Think he'll stick around?"

Mick nodded and looked at Keeley. "He said something to you, didn't he? What was it?"

She started. "I can't remember. It all happened so fast."

"Are you sure?" he pressed.

"Yes."

"I heard him speak to you."

John looped an arm around her shoulders. "She said no, didn't she?"

Keeley looked at the floor. "I'm really tired and I have to get up early."

"I'm going to have a patrol car drive by throughout the night, just as a precaution." The chief excused himself. "Staying in town, Mr. Hudson?"

Mick could see by the chief's sharp eyes that he was nobody's fool. It made him feel better. A little. "Not sure. Maybe I'll drive back home tonight."

Home? Was that what he had at the sanctuary? A home? It had begun to feel more and more like a hiding place. When he was ten he'd taken a dare and left school at lunchtime, climbing to the top of a fire lookout in the woods. His grandpa Phil had found him that day and took him right back to school, where he'd been made to write an apology to the teacher and sit with the first graders at lunchtime for a week. He'd towered over those kids, trying without success to scrunch down so he wouldn't be as obvious as Gulliver in the land of the Lilliputians.

"You can't hide from shame, Micky boy," his grandpa had said.

No, you can't, Grandpa.

When there was nothing left to say, Mick accepted a ride from Uttley back to his truck, parked a half mile from where he'd finally caught up with Keeley and Tucker.

Uttley was quiet for most of the trip, but Mick knew his wheels were turning.

"Got a call from Reggie Donaldson alerting us that Rivendale was likely on his way. Not time enough for us to do much."

Mick watched the moon glittering in brilliant streaks through the spires of the fir trees.

"So I get that this is personal." He cleared his throat. "I've been here awhile, so I was on the team that found LeeAnn. I wasn't the chief then. We were dispatched after Keeley got the text from her sister. I replay it in my mind all the time. I think if we'd found her sooner, if we got there quicker, we could have taken him into custody. More bad luck that your pal Reggie spotted him and tried to make the arrest. Tucker took him down, the car rolled into the pond, and he was long gone before we made it on scene." He huffed out a breath. "I had a bad feeling when we pulled that car out of the water, but I hoped it wasn't true. Kept right on hoping until we popped the trunk."

Reggie had told Mick later that the sight of Lee-Ann in that trunk would never leave his memory to his dying day. "It was as if she was staring at me, asking how we let it happen."

How had Mick let it happen? How had he been so completely fooled about Tucker's character?

Uttley shook his head. "Poor kid. LeeAnn was only guilty of loving the wrong guy. Never understood how girls could be so led by their hearts and not their heads."

Mick kept quiet.

Uttley tapped the steering wheel. "I've had situations that went bad, too. It stays with you. I understand. I know what it's like to believe in a parolee, to want them to succeed so much it blinds you to the facts."

There was something naked and raw in his tone that spoke of personal experience, but Mick knew cops, and they didn't share with people who didn't wear badges. Mick waited for the bottom line.

"But you're not a cop, and you make things worse by being here, so I'm glad you're going home."

Mick knew Uttley was right. Go home. Stay out of it. *It will only make things harder for the family I've already ruined.*

Still, he wondered as he thanked Uttley and gunned the engine on his truck.

What had Tucker said to Keeley back there in the darkness?

And why had she chosen not to tell the police about it?

I want what's mine. Had Tucker really said it? Did he really know? She'd not heard correctly. That was all. Her mind played a vile trick on her.

Keeley could not dislodge the words from inside. Jaw tight, she finally convinced John to leave.

"I'm fine. The house is locked up. The police are increasing their patrols. I'll be at the vet clinic tomorrow evening to help with the birds for a couple of hours."

"Keeley, it's okay to admit you're scared. Why don't you take some time off? Let me cook for you, or we can go for a walk."

She shook her head. "Thank you, but I need to work." Did she ever. The tiny house was hers after LeeAnn's death, but debt circled around her like a flock of ravenous crows. It was another ten days until the check would arrive, that mysterious check that showed up in time to save her, or so it seemed, every month.

"John, you don't, I mean, you don't, um, send me anything in the mail, do you?" She watched him closely for any flicker of emotion that would give him away.

"The mail? No. Why?"

"No reason." Part of her breathed a sigh of relief.

John could be lying—maybe he really was her mysterious benefactor—but she was happy that he did not appear to be guilty of that generosity. LeeAnn had left a hole in John's heart, even though she'd never done the smallest thing to encourage his affections, and he tried to assuage the ache by caring for Keeley. It won't work, she wanted to tell him. Nothing will take that pain away. It was uncomfortable to watch him try. And she certainly had no intention of being anything other than a friend to John, a fact that she'd made crystal clear, or so she hoped.

She succeeded in escorting him out the door.

"Please call me if there's anything at all that you need," he said.

"I will. Thank you."

She bolted the door behind him. For a moment, she leaned against the wood and let the quiet wash over, whispering a prayer of thanks that she had survived her face-to-face encounter with Tucker Rivendale. It was not so much for her physical safety she was grateful, but for the fact that her soul was still intact. So much rage coursed through her when she thought of him. For so long she'd worried that her desire for vengeance might just lead her to losing herself if she ever confronted him.

But she'd faced him; she'd stood inches from Tucker Rivendale, the man who killed her sister, and she was still standing.

And still filled with a black and roiling anger that

she knew would never dissipate. Where had the old Keeley gone? The fun-loving, curious athlete who found paths to hike where there were none? Who traveled the country to photograph birds, those unfettered kings of the sky? She remembered her sister's laughter, the way she would throw back her chin and let loose her joy in big belly chuckles at Keeley's antics. "I miss you, LeeAnn. I was a better person when you were here with me," she said to the empty room.

The next morning, when memories of the previous day ignited her anxiety, she applied the antidote and went for the duffel bag that had become her constant companion. Cameras, tripod, batteries, change of clothes, toiletries, a nearly empty wallet and a book. This time it was *What's New Boo Boo Bear?* At the secondhand store in town, she'd scored it for a dime.

Money couldn't buy happiness, but a well-spent ten cents could still get you some fun.

When everything was carefully stowed, she considered the time, nearly ten o'clock. She wasn't expected at Aunt Viv's until the afternoon.

"There are plenty of things I can do here," she said aloud to beat back the heavy silence. Shelves could be dusted. Another endless round of magazine queries could and should be sent out. At the very least, she should go to the hardware store and install an extra lock on the front and back doors.

But the flat emptiness in Tucker's eyes stirred a deep longing inside her that could only be counteracted by a certain bright cobalt gaze. Locking the door behind her, Keeley headed for the Jeep.

She drove out of Silver Creek, the small town of no more than five hundred people, past John's vet clinic. His lights were on. No surprise. He was probably the hardest-working man she'd ever met. Each stoplight and every mile covered lifted her spirits a little. Everything was okay, she told her unsettled nerves.

Tucker wouldn't dare return with the police out looking for him. Likely he would actually be caught this time, and she would have the pleasure of watching him sent to prison permanently like he should have been before.

Again her mind tried to fill in the details of Lee-Ann's final day. LeeAnn had gone to check on a wounded bird on the top of an abandoned warehouse and somewhere along the way she'd met up with Tucker. A couple of hours after her departure, she was dead in the trunk of Tucker's car, submerged in a pond. Not dead from drowning, but from a massive blow to the back of the head.

And Tucker? The man LeeAnn had believed in despite his criminal past? The man she'd taken up with again after he'd proved himself a louse? He'd been running when he'd crashed his car into a pond, and nearly arrested by an off duty Reggie Donaldson.

And where had Mick been in all this? Vacationing on his family's property in the mountains. Oblivious to the fact that he'd vouched for a would-be killer and had Tucker's tracking bracelet removed, a device that might have saved LeeAnn's life that day. She wanted to hate Mick Hudson, but something about the way he'd stared at her inexplicably twisted her feelings. The big brute of a man was intimately familiar with grief. It was carved into the lines of his face.

The road out of town smoothed out, straight and empty. Big Pines was larger and more populated, with easy access to doctors, therapists and a very special preschool. A glimmer of movement caught her eye in the rearview mirror. Her heart dropped for a moment as she imagined Tucker's motorcycle behind her.

"No, you ninny," she told herself. "Just the regular ebb and flow of lunchtime traffic heading to and from Big Pines." A black SUV with tinted windows pulled up closer and passed. Fingers tight on the wheel, her gut began the "what if" game.

If Tucker had eluded the police and stolen a car...

If he was determined to snatch the one thing, the only thing left of LeeAnn...

If he found out about Aunt Viv and where she lived...

She fought down the stampeding thoughts and pressed the gas pedal a little harder.

Arriving some forty minutes later, Keeley parked

a block from the house and sat, watching the cars drive by. Nothing unusual, no sign of anything out of the ordinary for a sleepy suburb.

Walking faster with each step, she made it to Aunt Viv's, knocked once and let herself inside, calling out a greeting.

Four toddlers looked up from their snack of apple slices and milk, which Aunt Viv was busily dispensing.

One little face with round cheeks and heavy-lidded eyes made her heart skip.

"Where's my June?" she called.

The little girl wriggled her short legs and flung an apple slice into the air in her excitement. She did not speak, but Keeley saw it all in her eyes.

"Hello, Mama," those luminous blue eyes seemed to say. The copper Brushfield spots in her irises, a hallmark of Down syndrome, twinkled like stars in a sapphire sky.

With a heart full of both joy and sorrow, Keeley went to embrace her.

THREE

Mick did his afternoon chores at the sanctuary in spite of the pain. His body was tired, arms throbbing, ribs creaking, when he found himself at the kitchen table, sitting in front of a roast-beef sandwich for which he had no appetite. His father, Perry, joined him, wearing an old pair of sweats. Mick was glad his jacket hid the cut on his biceps. His father had endured a boatload of worry that started some twenty years ago when a child was abducted on their property. His sister, Ruby, had recently found evidence about the case that had nearly got her killed and Mick thrown in jail. But now Ruby was happily married to Cooper Stokes, and Perry was enjoying some well-deserved peace.

"Got the brush cleared?"

Mick nodded.

"Must be tired after your trip." Perry raised an inquiring eyebrow as he sat down at the sturdy kitchen table.

"Drove into Silver Creek to take care of some old business."

"Old business? Like Tucker Rivendale?"

Mick couldn't imagine how his father knew, but the man had been a competent private eye in his day. Old habits died hard, and sometimes not at all. "Yeah. He's still at large."

"Did you find him?"

"Got away, but LeeAnn's sister is safe." It hurt to say her name. "Cops are all over it. They want me out of the way."

Perry sipped some water he'd poured for himself. "Think he'll come back?"

"He'd be a fool to do that. Cops don't think he will."

"What does your gut tell you?"

Mick sighed. "Can't trust my gut anymore, Dad."

"You made a mistake."

Mick got up and stalked to the window, bracing his palms on the kitchen sink. Justice and judgment, two of the most critical leadership traits drilled in as he was molded into a marine. He'd failed at both.

And at being a husband, to complete the list.

"It was more than a small error in judgment. I believed that Tucker was on the straight and narrow, that his days of jacking cars and conning people were over. I knew deep down he wasn't prone to violence. My gut told me I could trust him, and

I convinced the parole board to release him from house arrest. I was wrong. Dead wrong."

"Too much blame for one man." His father walked over and put his glass in the sink. He gripped his son's shoulder. "Things are quiet around here for the next month. If you need to get away, do it."

"I'm okay." He sighed. "What's the smart thing to do, Dad?"

"Stay out of it, just like the cops said."

They locked gazes. *But it won't bring you peace*, his father's eyes added.

Perry gave Mick a final pat. When had his father's hands gotten so old and gnarled? Perhaps twenty years of repressed fear about what had happened to the child abducted from their property had accelerated the aging process. Mick would swallow glass before he added any more grief to his father's plate.

"And if you need my help in any way, ask."

"I will."

When he'd gone, Mick stared out at the forest that pressed in all around the old house. He wanted to run outside, deep into the woods, and lose himself in the pungent scent of pine and the comforting presence of birds overhead, but he forced himself to remain.

It took him an hour of pacing to make the decision. He scrawled a note on a torn piece of paper and put it under the coffeepot.

Be away for a few days. I'll call you tonight. Kiss Ruby for me.

He tossed a bag in the bed of the pickup and started the long drive back to Silver Creek. When he stopped for gas, he listened to a message on his phone.

"You're not answering, which means you're driving back to Silver Creek. I decided to take a couple of days off and do a little fishing. I'm staying at a buddy's cabin about six miles out of town on Wexler Road. Got a couch for you if you want it. Stay out of trouble."

Mick chuckled as he drove to the cabin. A little fishing? Reggie Donaldson was a near-professional bowler and an excellent marksman, but an outdoorsy type he wasn't. Mick knew that Reggie was also a guy who didn't let things go, and Tucker Rivendale had made a mistake attacking Reggie when he'd tried to arrest him. Mick was grateful. With Reggie's connections, they might be able to help the police lay their hands on the kid before he did any more harm.

Mick still wondered why Tucker had come back and what he'd said to Keeley that she refused to tell the police. Thoughts tumbled around in his mind until he arrived at the small wood-sided cabin. Reggie opened the door, soda and pepperoni-pizza slice in hand.

"'Bout time. What'd you do, crawl?"

Mick stepped inside. He almost let a surprised grunt escape his mouth when he saw his friend.

From under the ragged fringe of black bangs, where Reggie's left eye had been there was now a sunken spot, the eyelid shriveled around the gap. He saw Mick's expression and pulled the patch down over his eye. "Gets hot under there. Got to let it air sometimes."

Mick recovered his composure. "I knew Tucker injured you when you tried to collar him. I didn't realize…"

"Me, neither," Reggie said, retrieving another slice of pizza from the box and handing it to Mick. "When we scuffled, he gouged me in the eye with his pocketknife. Wound didn't heal. Infection got down in deep until there was no way to fix it."

"I'm sorry."

"Not half as sorry as Tucker's going to be when I catch up to him." Reggie's good eye glittered. "You know what they say," he said, voice soft and dangerous, "about an eye for an eye."

Mick had never realized how powerful his need for vengeance was until he saw his anger reflected in Reggie's good eye. Mick had not lost his vision, but Tucker had taken a part of him just the same. Forgiveness was not, nor would ever be an option, in spite of what his sister's well-meaning church pastor had told him.

Sorry, God. This one isn't worth forgiving.

Mick tried to pull his emotions in check. "Haven't seen you in a while. How's Nadine?"

Reggie sighed. "She left me."

"Again?"

"It's going on six months this time," he said, wiping his mouth. "She's playing hardball, threatened a divorce and everything, but I'm making progress. After this adventure, I'm going to book us a cruise."

Mick chuckled. "Might want to check with Nadine before you put your money down."

"She'll come around. She always does. I just have to apply some grease to the skids."

"Seems as though you greased the skids last time she left you. You bought her diamonds, didn't you?"

He lifted a shoulder. "Turns out they really aren't a girl's best friend, because she insisted I return them before she let me back in the house. The cruise will be better. Quality time and all that."

Mick figured he certainly had no better ideas where women were concerned, so he stayed quiet.

Reggie extracted a bunch of papers from a portfolio and slid them onto a banged-up coffee table with one corner missing. "The old paperwork. Trying to find some leads about where Tucker might crash, if he's got any friends or such-like."

"Did you find anything?"

"Yeah, I'm chasing that down. In the meantime, there's something here you should see, something I dug up about the sister."

"LeeAnn?"

"Yeah. A little tidbit that might explain why Tucker's come to call."

Mick felt a cold hand grasp at his heart as he took the papers from Reggie. "Am I going to like this?"

Reggie didn't smile this time. "Read it, Mick."

Keeley spent the day playing with June, relishing every word the three-year-old said and the ones Keeley imagined she was thinking. June didn't say more than a few words due to speech delays, but each one was precious, like the biblical apples of gold. The best thing for June's speech development turned out to be Cornelius, Aunt Viv's parrot. The plucky African gray eyed June with curiosity and called her "Junie Jo" in an exact imitation of Aunt Viv. Cornelius would sometimes infuriate June by commanding her to sit in the time-out chair. Today he was singing "Yankee Doodle" to the delight of the toddlers.

Late in the afternoon when the other three children had been picked up by their parents, Aunt Viv finally plopped down onto the sofa, her slim hips jostling the cushions and setting June into gales of laughter.

"She said *coffee* today," Aunt Viv said with a laugh. "I let her pour some creamer into my cup and it went everywhere, so now she says, 'coffee, oops!'" Viv stroked one of June's soft blond pigtails as the child examined the pages of the book Keeley had brought.

"How did the OT go?"

June had worked with Mrs. B., her occupational therapist, since before she was old enough to walk.

"She's trying hard to pedal that tricycle. Almost there." Viv looked Keeley over. "I'll say it again. If you want to live here, I've got a closet-size extra room with your name on it. Not the Ritz, but clean, more or less."

Keeley shot her a look. "Why are you bringing it up?"

"You've got that worried 'my paycheck might not be enough to get us to the end of the month' look on your face."

Keeley turned the page, and June leaned her head against Keeley's side. There was nothing more she'd like than to spend every moment with June. When LeeAnn gave birth, Keeley had been there through it all: the shock of finding out the baby had Down syndrome, the denial, anger and grief that followed. Keeley had paced miles around that small hospital room, each step bringing her deeper and deeper in love with her precious niece, those wondrous eyes with the beautiful flecks, the most perfect tiny mouth. Little did she know then that her role would change from auntie to mother when June was only a year and a half.

Tucker hadn't wanted the baby, had urged Lee-Ann to get rid of it and then promptly gotten himself into trouble with the law for stealing a car. A devastated LeeAnn had moved away to live with their mother in Colorado, never letting Tucker know she'd had their baby.

"Don't tell him," she'd begged. "Ever. He doesn't want her, and she shouldn't know her father is a criminal. Promise."

Promise. The entreaty still rang in her ears. Even when LeeAnn had moved back to Oregon and she and Tucker had patched things up, LeeAnn had not told him the truth, leading him to believe June was Keeley's. She'd waited and waited, to be sure Tucker was on the straight and narrow. She'd died still waiting. And now? Did Tucker have an idea? Had he figured out the truth about June?

I want what's mine...

She pulled June closer. The little girl discarded the book and climbed onto Keeley's lap, laying her plump cheek on Keeley's chest.

"I have to make a life for us, Aunt Viv," she said, rubbing circles on June's back. "I need to get my business established, and I can't take June with me on the shoots. By summer, if I take every job I can get my hands on, I'll be able to hire someone reliable to watch her while I'm working until she's ready to start the prekindergarten program."

Just the thought of it made little flutters roil through her stomach. Would the public school understand a special-needs child? Could they see past the label to the amazing, exquisite person underneath? Would she be teased and tormented by the other children?

"Just remember, it's an option if things get too hairy." Aunt Viv reached out her arms. "Give that little sweetie pie to me. She's sound asleep. I'll put her down for a nap."

Keeley smiled. She knew that meant Viv would lie down next to her and take a snooze, as well. Aunt Viv earned every moment of her rest time. The energetic fifty-five-year-old tended to four rambunctious preschoolers in her at home day care setting and toted June to her various appointments when Keeley was working. Since she'd retired from being an emergency room nurse when she'd moved to Colorado the year before, June had become her full-time work.

"I'll put some chicken in the oven for dinner," Keeley said.

"I won't be noble. You can cook for me anytime." She disappeared down the hallway, her long black braid trailing behind her.

After the chicken was seasoned with olive oil, a squeeze of lemon and a generous handful of crushed garlic, it went into the oven to bake. Keeley began gathering up the toys June and her friends had scattered about the playroom and swept and mopped the kitchen floor. Her phone indicated an email.

It was a request from a magazine she'd queried in the past. Short notice, but can you photograph the Quaker parrots? Our guy dropped out and we need it for a midnight deadline. Fred. Her pulse kicked up a notch. If she could deliver, it might mean steady work with *Bird's Away Magazine*.

Hurriedly, she emailed her acceptance and checked her phone. Four o'clock. She'd have just enough time to drive to the industrial part of town the colony of feral parrots called home and take some pictures before sunset.

She tiptoed into the bedroom and found Aunt Viv snoring softly. June was rolled into a ball sleeping next to her. Something warm and soft settled into Keeley's heart.

"Thank You, God," she said for the millionth time. Nothing would ease the pain of what Tucker had done to LeeAnn, but there was June, sweet June. Each word she spoke was balm to Keeley's broken heart, every boisterous laugh salve to the pain.

Keeley knew that every job brought her closer to being the mommy that LeeAnn would have wanted for her precious child. Keeley closed the door quietly. She packed up her gear while the chicken finished cooking, and left it cooling on the counter with a note.

"Job! Wild parrots. Back in a couple of hours. Save me some chicken. K."

She sent a text to John, telling him she would not volunteer at the clinic that evening. It gave her a sense of relief, she was ashamed to admit. She'd taken over LeeAnn's volunteer role of tending to the wild birds John rescued. LeeAnn had loved the birds so much, but being around John meant Keeley would feel both his pain as well as her own. It was too much.

She tiptoed out the door and hustled to her Jeep, stopping short as she saw Mick Hudson leaning on her front bumper. He straightened as he saw her approach.

Her stomach somersaulted. How had he known to find her here? She forced a calm pace until she reached him.

"I thought you'd left town," she said.

"Came back." His gaze made her squirm, as if he knew all her secrets.

"What do you want?"

"Tucker did say something to you out there on the mountain, and you kept it to yourself."

Her cheeks burned. "Things happened fast. I can't really recall exactly…"

"Do you have reason to think Tucker knows the child is his?"

The words sucked the breath right out of her, and cold gripped her body. She tried to go around him. "I don't know what you're talking about."

He put a hand on her shoulder, heavy, strong.

"Yes, you do. The little girl your sister gave birth to. Tucker's the father, isn't he?"

"Who do you think you are?" she said, fear sparked into anger as she yanked out of his grip. "Coming into my life and spouting accusations and prying into private information that you have no right to. June is mine, I'm her legal guardian and her biological father is none of your business."

"It's Tucker's business. He's come back to take her and punish you."

Coming for you.

Ice spread throughout her body. "June is my daughter."

"You need to tell the police."

"Tucker's gone. He's taken off."

"Sure about that?"

The flat brown eyes, the arms folded across the broad chest infuriated her. "You have no right to interfere. You're not a cop."

"I'm trying to help."

"The time to help was when Tucker should have been under house arrest. You helped then, didn't you? You made sure he was a free man, and then he killed my sister." The wide river of anger flowed out of her and caused him to flinch. He looked away. She would not, could not, stop. "The one thing I want more than anything else in this world is my sister back, but you can't help with that, can you?" Her throat thickened.

"I...don't want to cause you any more pain."

"Then go away."

He bent down and picked up a penny-size round bead. "This looks important."

How did he know that black bead was super important to a certain little girl? "It belongs to Junie's toy cow, Mr. Moo Moo." She quickly snatched the bead and stashed it in her pocket. "Thank you," she managed.

"I don't think Tucker is leaving until he gets what he wants."

She rekindled her anger. He was not about to push his way into her life or parenting decisions. "Why should it matter what you think, Mr. Hudson?" She stalked to the driver's-side and got in, pulling away without looking in the rearview mirror, though she could feel him standing there, watching. Her hands were clammy as she gripped the steering wheel.

He's come back to take her and punish you.

Mick's ominous words would not leave her mind as she drove to the old warehouse in the industrial part of town. Could he be right? Could Tucker have figured out that June was his child? Why would he care anyway? When LeeAnn had told him about the pregnancy, he'd pushed her to end it immediately. He had not wanted a baby then. And now? That he was a fugitive with a target on his back?

Oh, why had her sister ever come back to Silver Creek? She and June might be living a happy life together if LeeAnn and Tucker had never rekindled their deadly relationship.

Her worries only increased with every mile until she finally called the police. It reassured her to hear that they had instituted roadblocks and had their eyes on train stations and the bus depot, and that the frequent neighborhood patrols would continue.

Should she tell them about June? She'd promised LeeAnn never to reveal the truth about June's parentage, but if Mick was right, Keeley was putting the child at risk by not breaking her vow. She had to trust someone with the truth. Her stomach churned.

She made arrangements to meet with Chief Uttley at seven, leaving her just enough time to do her job. Was it the right choice or wrong? She had no idea, so she squashed the whirling anxiety and focused on the task at hand.

Her quarry would be best photographed at the top of the empty six-story building, once the home of the *Oregon Weekly Tribune*. The building stood resolutely against the sinking sun, as if guarding the colony of bright green Quaker parrots that had set up residence on the roof of the neighboring storage facility. The ingenious avian builders had infiltrated every nook and cranny, stuffing each crevice with a mountain of twigs to build their enormous communal nests. From her vantage point, with the zoom lens, Keeley could get incredible shots of the master builders at work.

Keeley climbed up the fire-escape ladders of the newspaper building, one arduous flight after the other, until she arrived, panting, at the top. Cold wind assaulted her cheeks. The rooftop was littered with detritus, broken branches, feathers that had been carried by the breeze and deposited against the ventilation boxes and piles of weathered pallets, stacked in six-foot piles in haphazard fashion. A flicker of motion made her jump.

She heaved out a sigh as a parrot waddled out from behind a crate, a long stick held in his beak. "Wrong building, bird," she said, snapping his picture anyway. He took off, flying toward the communal nest.

After one more cautious look around, Keeley settled herself onto her stomach, her camera steadied on a tiny tripod. She zoomed the lens and took a couple of test shots to check the lighting.

Perfect. She reveled as she always did in the privilege of being able to peek into a hidden world, a secret place, and document the wild lives burgeoning around her.

A parrot with puffy white cheeks and brilliant emerald feathers alighted to preen on the ledge of the adjacent building. Keeley readied her camera.

"Hold still, birdie. One more second," she whispered.

The scuff of a shoe behind her made her whirl around, heart thundering in her chest.

"You sound just like your sister," Tucker Rivendale said.

FOUR

Mick called Reggie on the way.

"I just got word from my source that he's been holing up at that newspaper building," Reggie sniped into the phone as Mick drove after Keeley. "I'm on my way there right now. Please don't tell me Keeley is headed there, too."

Mick had followed Keeley long enough to realize that for some reason that he could not fathom, that was exactly where she seemed to be going. "Can't ease your mind on that count."

"And you're right behind her." Reggie sighed. "At least you're armed."

Mick remained silent.

"You don't have a gun?" Reggie thundered. "How are you gonna take him out before he kills the girl?"

How many times after he'd left the marines had he found himself reaching for a gun when a car backfired or a stranger approached just a little too quickly? Which was exactly why he'd promised himself he'd never again carry one.

"You've gotta keep her off that rooftop until I get there. You stay off, too."

"I'm pulling up in the parking lot right now." Mick disconnected. Keeley's car was there, but no sign of her. He raced to the front and rattled the doors—locked. What would her second move be? Same as his, the fire escape. He hastened to the nearest set of ladders. The rusted metal scraped at his fingers, the rungs creaked under his weight as he took the first step.

Two rungs up and a voice called out, "Hey." Fingers grabbed at his calf.

He whirled and barely had time to check his reflexive kick as he jumped down. It was the vet guy. John something or other.

John's eyes were narrowed into suspicious slits. "What are you doing here?"

Mick's first rule: never give away any information unless strictly necessary. "Not your business."

"If you're here because of Keeley, it is my business." John stepped between him and the ladder.

Mick did not want to take the time. "Can't talk now. Get out of my way."

"And what if I don't?"

He sighed. "Look. If you want to fight, we'll do it later. Right now, I have reason to believe Keeley is heading for trouble. Move, or I'll have to go through you."

John's lips tightened, but he did as Mick demanded. Smart.

"Should I call the police?" he yelled up.

Mick's second rule: never waste time answering a question that someone already knew the answer to. Mick left him to stew over that decision as he raced up the ladder. Back in the day as a young marine, he could have made the climb easily. Now, in spite of his rigorous fitness regimen, his knee, torn and abused over the years, complained after the second floor. He pressed on.

One more flight and he was at the top. He risked a quick look and his heart lurched. Keeley stood next to Tucker Rivendale. When Tucker caught a glimpse of Mick, he darted an arm around her throat, the blade of a knife held under her jaw. She looked more perplexed than scared.

"Come on up, Mick," Tucker called. "Might as well make this a party."

Mick stepped onto the roof. "Did he hurt you?" he asked Keeley.

"You never did trust me, did you?" Tucker said, with a laugh.

"I did, and that was a mistake I won't make again."

"Maybe it's her you should be doubting." He squeezed Keeley around the shoulders. She flinched. Tucker shook his head. "She's a liar, you know. She's lied to me for three years now, trying to take my kid."

Keeley stiffened. "June isn't yours. You never wanted her. You killed LeeAnn, and you don't deserve to be a father."

Tucker's eyes went wide. "I'm guilty, huh, end of story? You get to decide that I don't have the right to be a father to my own kid?"

"Let her go, Tucker," Mick said. "You killed that little girl's mother. In my book, that strips your dad status."

"Everyone in this world is a dirty liar." Tucker pushed Keeley away and she sprawled on the rooftop. Mick edged closer, between Keeley and Tucker. Now she had a chance; the playing field was more level. There was no way to win a knife fight without some serious bloodshed, but he could hold Tucker off long enough for Keeley to scramble down from the fire escape.

Tucker's mouth twisted. "Listen, man. I know you've been helping them all this time to find me."

"True. You're a murderer, you deserve to be incarcerated."

"I deserve plenty, but not the blame for killing LeeAnn."

Mick grunted. "Save me the sob story. You're going to prison where you belong."

Tucker pointed the knife at Mick, eyes narrowed. "I thought you were different."

"Because I was gullible enough to be manipulated by you?" Shame flooded his insides until he shut it down. "Take your best shot, Tucker. You're only going to get one."

"Don't want it to be this way." Tucker weighted back on his heels, crouched low.

Mick did the same, hoping his reflexes were a match for his younger opponent. He had plenty of hand-to-hand combat training, but his arm still throbbed from the wound Tucker had given him before. If he'd had a gun, as Reggie supposed he did…

Something sailed through the air and over Tucker's head. He jerked as Keeley reached for another bit of broken wood that littered the rooftop and hurled it as fast as she could, fury convulsing her face. Her aim wasn't good. Many of them plunked into Mick's shoulders and one struck him in the cheek, but it was enough to get Tucker off balance.

As Tucker raised an arm to shield his face, Mick reached to pull her away.

A gunshot exploded from behind the pile of pallets.

Mick launched himself at Keeley and brought her to the ground, covering his body with hers as another shot sent bits of the concrete roof flying through the air. The bullets sent the parrots on the next building into a cacophony of panicked squawks and flapping wings. The air was alive with green feathery bodies.

When the shots died away, he dared to lift his head and look up. Tucker was not visible from his line of sight. He scrambled to his feet and took

Keeley's hand, pulling her around the back side of a ventilation duct, some small protection from whoever was unloading bullets in their direction.

Keeley sucked in a breath, face dead white. "Is someone trying to help? Or are they aiming for us?"

Mick's face betrayed the same disbelief that Keeley was sure hers did, only he showed no trace of the wild fear that beat in her own heart. There was only rage in the taut lines of his jaw and lips. He held her wrist tightly, almost painfully so, crouched as if to leap up at any moment. "Stay here," he whispered.

"Okay. My legs have turned to rubber anyway," she whispered back.

His lips quirked for a moment. Then he was gone.

Keeley pressed close to the air duct, trying to steady her quivering muscles. She could hear the parrots still screeching from the nearby trees at the violation of their nesting area. She felt as if hers had been violated, too. First Tucker, appearing like a horrible nightmare, and then some crazy rooftop shooter. Was she dreaming? No, the convulsive squeeze of her panicked heart was all too real.

Where was Tucker? Even now, was he circling around behind her with his knife? She scooped up a board knocked loose from one of the pallets. It would have to do. If he wanted to kill her like he had her sister, she sure wasn't going to make it easy for him.

The sound of running feet made her breath hitch. She readied the board. Mick appeared around the corner, a trickle of blood running from the wound on his cheek. Something had changed in the stern lines of his mouth. "Come on out."

"But…" She found she was talking to his back as he strode toward the spot where Tucker had been moments before.

A dark-haired man with an eye patch stood there, one hand on his hip and the other still gripping his gun.

Mick bore down on the man, seeming larger in his anger, his wide shoulders like the prow of a battleship.

"You could have hit her, Reggie," he snarled. His voice didn't grow louder, but the man shrank back a pace.

"Not my fault."

"Your finger on the trigger, your fault."

Reggie shook his head and swore.

"And Tucker's gone," Mick added. "Made it down the back fire escape. Took off on his motorcycle. What were you thinking?"

"Please." Reggie snorted. "Blame me if it makes you feel better, but I hauled myself up three flights of a fire-escape ladder because you are too thickheaded to carry a weapon. I made it up here in time to see Tucker with a knife and then Keeley starts throwing stuff, so I have two seconds to squeeze off a clean shot, only Wonder Boy messes it up."

"Who...?" Mick started.

Keeley was flabbergasted to see John emerge from behind a ventilation duct holding a half-empty bag of pretzels between his fingertips. John's eyes were wide with shock. "Tucker's been hanging out here, on this roof."

"You don't say," Reggie spat. "What I want to know is who you are and why did you interfere?"

John blinked. He looked at Keeley. "Are you okay?"

She was going to answer, but Reggie broke in. "No thanks to you. You dived at me. I could have killed her or Mick."

John flushed. "I saw you start up the ladder. I didn't know who you were. I followed you up and saw you take out a gun. What was I supposed to think?"

"Aww, man." Reggie jammed his gun into the holster. "It doesn't explain what you're doing here in the first place. Who are you anyway? Maybe you're working with Tucker, huh? Maybe you had a reason you didn't want me to shoot the kid."

"I'd be happy to let you shoot him," John said.

"Then explain yourself before I throttle you," Reggie shouted.

Mick raised his palms. "Let him speak his piece."

"I'm Dr. John Bender. I'm a veterinarian, and I've known Keeley and her sister for a long time.

I called Aunt Viv's house to check on Keeley. Viv told me Keeley took a job photographing the parrots. There's only one place you're going to find parrots around here, so I knew where she was going."

"But why did you follow me?" Keeley watched a wary look settle into his eyes.

"I thought you might need someone to keep tabs on you, with Rivendale back in town." His chin went up. "I was right, too. Tucker might have killed you."

"I might have killed her, thanks to you," Reggie snapped. "You need to stay out of this, Doc. Am I making myself crystal clear?"

John stiffened. "Are you a cop?"

"Parole officer, and I know Tucker Rivendale well. Very well."

"I know him well, too." John leaned closer until the two men were close, glaring into each other's faces. "He murdered the woman I loved."

Reggie cocked his head. "I get that, and you're desperate to be a man and be all protective and such, but you're going to get yourself into trouble by poking your nose in. Stick to the animals, Doc."

John started to fire off a retort until Keeley put her hand on his shoulder. "I know you meant well coming after me. Thank you."

He broke off staring at Reggie to give her a nod. "I'm glad you're okay. I would never put you

in harm's way. You know that, right?" He took
her hands.

"Yes." Keeley gave his fingers a squeeze and
then detached her hands from his.

"While you were down there, did you call the
cops?" Mick said to John.

John shook his head. "I decided to investigate
first. I'll do that right now." He stepped away a few
paces and dialed his phone.

Reggie stalked away to examine the rooftop.

Silence stretched between her and Mick until she
grew uneasy. "I'm, um, sorry I hit you," Keeley
said, pointing to the gash on Mick's face. "Seems
like I'm either running over you or clobbering you
with something."

"No problem." He smiled, and the action lit up
the satin depths of his eyes, a transformation she
never would have thought possible. It swept away
the flicker of what she hadn't recognized before.
Under the anger, he had been afraid, but not for
himself. For her. Why? Maybe because he hadn't
been fearful enough about Tucker, about what he
was capable of doing to her sister. The ache spiraled
afresh, pounding a trail through her nerves. If he'd
only been more worried about what Tucker might
do before he got the tracking device removed. "I've
got some Band-Aids in the car, but I think they
might have rubber duckies on them."

"I'll pass, but thank you." The lightness left. "I'm
going to check something out. Stay here."

The irritation rose again. Stay here. Do this. Go here. He was very free with the directions for a guy that she didn't invite into her life and never would. *I call the shots in my life, Mick. Get that straight.* Mick went to the far side of the building and climbed down the fire escape. She hugged herself, watching Reggie prowl the rooftop, scowling. John appeared to be finishing up his phone call.

Dead leaves skittered across the roof. The faraway distressed call of the birds still drifted on the wind. Her heart returned, as it always did, to June. Junie, precious child. What was she doing right now? Playing with clay? Using her chubby fingers to create wild paintings of scenes in bold stripes of red and yellow? Had she noticed Mr. Moo Moo was missing an eye? She allowed herself for one moment to imagine what her life would be like if Junie was suddenly snatched away, gone without so much as a goodbye embrace, like LeeAnn had been. Bile rose in her throat, pulse edging upward with the horror and shaking her courage. Who could she trust to get her out of the mess? *No one. You're going to have to do it yourself, so stop letting everyone order you around.*

She found herself following Mick's path down the fire escape.

John called something out to her, but she didn't stop. All her energy was spent in keeping her sanity; she had nothing left over to handle John's immense sadness or the animosity between him,

Reggie and Mick. The ladder rungs bit into her palms, but she welcomed the movement, pain and all. One flight down and she realized there was an open window, halfway ajar, through which Mick must have squeezed.

She fit through the opening easily, emerging on a dusty floor in a large open area crowded with broken office chairs and more wooden pallets. The far corner had one small office with a dust-smeared window. Mick was on one knee near a long-abandoned file cabinet, examining something.

He looked up at her approach.

"I know, I didn't stay as ordered, but honestly I can't. First, bossing people around is not polite, and second, inactivity is just not in my physiology. You can ask all my teachers from over the years."

His mouth quirked. "Let me guess. PE was your favorite class?"

"Yes."

"Mine, too."

Enough of the pleasantries. She peered closer. "What did you find?"

He pointed to a sleeping bag. "Tucker's been crashing here. Couple of empty food cans, eaten recently. This is what puzzles me." With a discarded piece of wire he found on the floor, Mick pulled a piece of crumpled paper loose. It was a diagram of some sort. Keeley looked closer.

"Is that the rooftop?"

"Yes." Mick frowned. "Why would Tucker be so

interested in the rooftop of an abandoned newspaper office?"

Keeley's stomach tightened. "And a building not more than one mile from where the police recovered his car with my sister's body in the trunk. What does it mean?"

"I don't know. Yet."

Something about the last word worried her. Mick would keep digging, which means he would stick in her life like a thorn. *Just find out the truth and he'll be gone.* She poked a toe at a pile of empty snack-cake wrappers, muscles tensing. "Mick…"

He stood. "Uh-huh?"

She stared at the wrappers, sticky with icing. "My sister never could understand how Tucker had no sweet tooth whatsoever. She always told me it was unnatural."

They locked eyes.

With the wire, he teased a receipt out of a discarded plastic grocery bag. "Purchased last night at a Pick and Pack a couple of miles from here." He squinted at the time stamp. "Just after eleven."

Cold trickled down her spine. "I have a feeling Tucker has someone helping him."

"Gonna keep looking," he said.

He pushed open the door of the office. She was about to follow him inside when out of the corner of her eye she caught the blur of movement, followed by the crash of the stairwell door being flung open behind her.

FIVE

In a moment, Mick shot out of the office and tore after the figure, Keeley pounding along right behind. As he slammed into the stairwell, he stumbled over a pile of boxes that the fugitive had flung across the stairs to slow their progress.

He heaved them out of the way, but it cost him precious time. Whoever it was took the stairs, as fleet as a deer. He pounded down, flinging the bottom-floor exit door open, blinking in the sunlight.

A deputy looked up from his radio, hand reflexively moving toward his gun. Mick stopped and raised his palms. "Mick Hudson. Behind me is Keeley Stevens. We found someone hiding inside the building. Did you see anyone exit just now?"

"No," Chief Uttley said, coming around the corner. "I heard the door crash open and I went to investigate while Officer Mason radioed the info."

Mick raised an eyebrow. "You didn't see anyone come out?" From Mason's vantage point, he could not imagine how he'd missed a fleeing figure who would have had to cross thirty feet of open space before disappearing around the neighboring building and into the forest beyond.

"I said no," Uttley repeated. "Am I correct, Mason?"

Mason remained silent after a short nod.

The hostility was clear to Mick. "We found some evidence that Tucker's been holed up inside with someone else."

Uttley shrugged. "Nice dry place, warm. Good spot for homeless people to hang out. That's probably it."

"I don't…"

Uttley's volume edged up a notch. "Mr. Hudson, you've forgotten our earlier agreement. You were going to get out of Silver Creek and leave the law enforcement to the people qualified to do that job." He tapped his chest. "The ones with badges."

Heat rose to Mick's cheeks. The part that had gotten him in trouble his whole life flared up again—the stubborn, prideful side of his soul that would not be talked down to. It had been the hardest challenge to becoming a marine, taking orders, letting someone break you down bit by bit. But in this case, Uttley was right. He was not the marine, not a parole officer, just a civilian. "I didn't intend to butt in."

"Yet you did, so I'll ask you politely now to butt out. Next time, it won't be a request." He turned to his deputy. "I'll go check it out and photograph everything. Keep everyone here until we get initial statements."

Mason nodded, and Mick and Keeley walked toward Reggie and John, who stood in stony silence next to Chief Uttley's police car.

Keeley gave Mick a sidelong glance. "Uttley's not a fan of yours."

"He's got plenty of company, then." Mick stopped a few yards away and turned to her, noting that she seemed only a touch winded by their flight down the stairs. "Keeley, why did you come here, to the newspaper building? Now?"

"I got a text from a man named Fred at *Bird's Away Magazine*. The email said he needed the picture, ASAP." She frowned. "Do you think Tucker sent it?"

"Let me see the text." He copied the number from her phone. The setting sun caught the soft curve of her cheeks, the frown that drew her delicate brows together. He did not see a shadow of hatred in her eyes, behind the pain and fear and he wondered why. "Keeley, until the cops catch him…"

She shook her head, face suddenly hard. "Don't say it."

"June isn't safe."

He knew those three words were the worst she could hear. *June isn't safe.* How could it be that any human being could threaten an innocent child? He couldn't understand it, even though his own family had been torn apart when a child was abducted right under their noses. Children did not deserve to have their lives messed up by adults. His mind flew back in time. He thought about his son's tiny grave, recalled the feel of a cold headstone under his fingertips, his memory mingled with the scent of carnations, which he could not abide to this day. "I'm sorry," he said lamely. "To have to say it."

Keeley blinked, folded her arms tight across her chest. He readied himself for the angry rant he knew was coming. Instead she began to shudder, eyes closed as if the world was spinning around her. Silent sobs shook her body. He caught her forearms, pulling her to his chest to keep her from falling.

"Deep breaths," he murmured, tightening his embrace, grazing his mouth against her soft hair.

"I don't know what's wrong with me," she whispered.

He heard her teeth chattering, and he tightened his embrace, pressing his cheek to the top of her head as if he could infuse what strength he had into her. "Delayed shock," he said. "It's okay. You're entitled."

John arrived, stopping so abruptly he skidded on the loose debris. "What is it? Were you hurt after all?" He pushed close to her and Mick let go, taking off his jacket and handing it to John, who snatched it and draped it over Keeley's shoulders. "We'll get you to the ER."

She breathed hard for a few moments, forcing

her features into a state of control. Strong woman, in spite of her slight stature. Reminded him of his sister, Ruby.

"I don't need the hospital."

"Yes, you do. Please be sensible," John said firmly, brushing the hair from her face. Mick agreed with John for once, but he wasn't about to share that sentiment.

"No," she said sharply. "I know what's best for me."

John flinched. "I'm sorry." He looked away, squinting at the sky. "I was overbearing. I just... My mind wants to rewind, to do things over again the right way. If I'd been more forceful about my feelings..."

The regret in John's voice repelled Mick. He took a step away. Shame wasn't something a man trotted out for all the world to see.

Keeley sighed. "LeeAnn knew how you felt."

John shook his head, hand still on her back. "I meant my feelings about him."

Mick caught the bile that dripped from the last word. "About Tucker?"

John didn't answer, but Mick saw the look on Keeley's face as she studied him.

"Dr. Bender," Mason called. "Would you mind answering a few questions now?"

John squeezed Keeley around the shoulders, pressed a kiss to her temple and trudged off.

Mick stared after him, and Reggie, who had sauntered closer, did, too.

"Guy's a coiled spring," Reggie said. "Must have had it bad for LeeAnn."

Mick watched Keeley, whose eyes changed from blue to pewter in the shifting rays of sun. "I wonder."

Reggie ran a thumb under his eye patch. "What?"

"John was so concerned about Keeley that he stopped me as I was on my way up, and then he risked getting himself shot by interrupting you."

"Yeah, so?"

"So if he was deeply concerned," Mick continued, "why did he wait so long to call the cops?"

Reggie considered. "Dunno. Doesn't trust them, maybe?"

I'm not sure I do, either, Mick thought.

Chief Uttley joined them. "Photographed everything, took the roof diagram, but in my opinion Tucker's been staying here alone. There's some other trash, but it's old."

"But…" Keeley said.

Uttley cut her off and looked at Reggie. "Mr. Donaldson, I'm looking forward to hearing your part in this messy little encounter. There will be a nice bit of paperwork to go through, especially since you discharged your weapon twice. We'll secure the scene and drive back to the station. I trust that won't ruin your plans?"

"Nah," Reggie said with an airy wave. "I've got

to call my travel agent and book a cruise, but it can wait." He winked at Keeley and headed for his car. "Catch you later, Mick." His tone hardened, probably imperceptibly to anyone, but not to Mick. "We've got some things to talk over."

Understatement. Mick still burned inside at Reggie's negligence. He was so bent on revenge that he was willing to endanger Keeley. Mick was going to have to keep tabs on that escalating problem.

Further, Mick was going to have to figure out why Uttley was protecting whoever was holed up in the building with Tucker. But the bigger issue at the moment was, who had sent the text that delivered Keeley to the rooftop? Was it Tucker, or did he have someone else helping him?

Keeley's knees were still shaking, but she insisted on driving herself to the police station. She wanted to be away from Reggie and John and, most important, from Mick, to sort out her feelings. How was a person supposed to put their emotions in order after being cornered by their sister's killer and told her child was the real target?

She gripped the wheel and used the hands-free phone to dial Aunt Viv.

"The police have already been here," Aunt Viv reassured her. "They're not anyone I know, I think they're on loan from another department, but the chief is coming later." She shushed Cornelius, who loved to chatter away when she was on the phone.

"I think Cornelius knows I'm taking him for a wing and nail trim soon. It's not his favorite thing."

She knew her aunt had a tendency to rattle on when she was overwrought. "Aunt Viv, are you and June okay?"

"Yes," she said. "Our lives are perfectly normal except for the police car parked outside. They said we're completely safe. They came inside to check all the locks and such, too. So embarrassing. I hadn't gotten around to dusting in the family room for ages, and my violin sheet music was all over the study."

Keeley smiled through her worry. "I don't know what's going to happen." Her voice wobbled.

"Honey," her aunt said quietly. "It's going to be okay. Junie is safe and so are you. That's all that matters. God's watching out for you."

It was a sentiment she wanted desperately to believe, but the knowledge of what happened to LeeAnn kindled new fear inside her. No one was completely safe. Ever. She could accept that for her own life, but not for June, and she would do anything in her power to protect her daughter. "I'll come when I'm done with the police."

"Umm, now don't get upset, but they told me you shouldn't visit for a few days, just until they make sure about things, in case Tucker's following you."

Keeley's eyes filled. She'd had a feeling it was coming but the words cut like glass. "I can't... I'm not allowed to see her?"

"Just for a few days," Viv crooned. "Derek knows what he's doing."

Derek Uttley? "I didn't know you were on a first name basis."

Viv sighed. "Honey, I'm retired. That doesn't mean I don't have a social life."

Keeley knew her aunt had met Uttley when her car was stolen a few short weeks after she moved to Silver Creek following LeeAnn's murder. She wanted to ask some questions, but despair clogged up her mind.

"We can Skype as many times as you want. I've told my other clients that I have to take some time off for the next week, and I arranged for the kids to go to another day care, just to be on the safe side."

So Aunt Viv's business was now affected, too. Tucker had the power to hurt everyone she loved. Keeley swallowed the burn that crept from her stomach into her throat. "Okay," she whispered. "Just until we solve the problem."

Viv talked on for a while longer, but Keeley could not hear over the rushing in her own ears. She felt the same sick desire take hold again as it had the moment she'd heard about LeeAnn, the need to clutch the steering wheel, stomp the gas and drive as far and fast as she could.

You're not a mother, Keeley.

You don't know what to do.

Panic, hot and acidic, bubbled inside as she fought the urge to run away.

God will not call you to do something He hasn't equipped you for. Her sister had scrawled it on the bathroom mirror with lipstick after June was born, and they had both read it over and over. But He'd done just that, hadn't He? Keeley was not ever planning to have kids of her own, and now here she was, mother to her sister's baby, and a child with special needs at that.

Her fingers grew slick with cold sweat as she gripped the wheel, struggling with her own internal darkness.

"Keeley? Are you still there?"

She forced in a breath and shoved away the panic. "Yes, I'm here."

"Okay. You sort of faded away for a moment."

Faded away into a place she must not allow herself to go. June needed her. God would give her the strength. She might not be the best stand-in for a mother, but she was only one June had. She wiped a shaking hand across her forehead. "Can I say good night to her?"

"Sure. She's pretty tired, though. All ready for bed."

"Wearing her pink jammies?" Keeley said through tears.

"Pink with the kitty on the front, her favorite. I have to quickly launder them during the day or she pitches a fit at bedtime." Aunt Viv put June on the line.

"Hey, Junie Jo," Keeley said, fighting for a serene tone.

June breathed noisily into the phone. "Hi, Mama."

"I—I can't come get you tonight. I'm sorry. But I'll see you real soon."

There was a soft sucking sound, and she imagined June slurping on her two fingers, as she'd done since shortly after her birth.

"Did you brush your teeth?"

"Uh-huh."

"Good girl. Say your prayers with Aunt Viv, okay?"

"Okay."

"Good night, Junie." She swallowed hard. "I love you."

"Love you, Mama."

Love you, Mama. Why did four simple syllables make every excruciating parenting moment fade away? All the arduous bouts of physical therapy, the endless doctor appointments and dizzying fears about money evaporated in the face of that pure sweetness.

Junie's speech had been a long time coming, thanks to her small oral cavity and high arched palate, as the doctors explained. For a long time, Junie's speech sounded like no more than babbling to Keeley, in spite of the endless games of peekaboo and the elaborate "mmm" after bites of dinner to encourage her to make the proper sounds.

Then, out of the blue, came "Mama." The first time she'd heard it on that day when June had just sent a dozen oranges cascading off the grocery store shelf, Keeley had fallen to her knees, clasping a startled June in a bear hug. Then she'd turned her face away to prevent June from seeing her anguished tears. The word, the precious syllables, should have been a gift to her sister, June's real mother.

She was a fraud, pretending to be a mother. Doubt, grief, fear, desperation, love.

Mama.

The loss rang through her again, like the clash of cymbals. She knew she would never stop missing her sister, and each gain of June's would remind her of what she'd lost. Every new word should be LeeAnn's to treasure; each ink mark on the doorjamb to measure another inch grown belonged to LeeAnn.

What would LeeAnn have done in the present circumstance? Fought Tucker with every breath, every last ounce of her courage; anything to save her daughter.

Junie, I will not let Tucker take you. The resolve hardened like marble in her heart. She wasn't a detective, or a parole officer, or a cop, but she had the only credential that mattered more. God had made her a mother, and that trumped everything else.

I will find him, baby, and he will never put his evil hands on you.

Doubt surged afresh. What could she do that the police couldn't? She had to be crazy.

"Just crazy enough," she whispered under her breath. "Love you, too, Junie Jo."

SIX

Mick was surprised when Keeley knocked on the window of his pickup truck in the police station parking lot. Reggie had finished up a half hour before and gone back to the cabin. Mick was also done being grilled by Uttley. He'd learned little except that the Fred at *Bird's Away Magazine* had not sent the text and that Uttley liked Mick even less than he had earlier.

Mick leaned over and opened the door for Keeley. She climbed in.

"You're waiting around to follow me home, aren't you?" she demanded.

Another question that didn't need an answer, but he nodded to be polite.

"This is crazy. I just explained to John that you're following me everywhere, and I do not need his protection or yours."

Not that the scrawny doctor-boy could help out much, Mick thought. "I told him that I'd be keeping you under watch until Tucker's caught."

She blew out a breath. "Fine. I'm not very skilled at shaking off tails, as they say in the movies, so I just thought I'd tell you right up front I'm not going home just yet. I'm going to the Pick and Pack."

He raised an eyebrow. "Urgent need for groceries?"

"No," she said, her voice hummed with a fierce current of determination.

The silence lengthened between them until she sighed. "I'm thinking you're going to know if I lie. I'm a terrible liar. My mother always knew when I was lying. She said my eyes turned silver. Are they silver now?"

He allowed a smile. "No, but maybe that's because you haven't started in on the lying part yet."

She sighed. "I can't be with June until Tucker is in jail."

He waited.

She stared him full in the face. "You don't talk much, do you?"

"Never had much to say."

"Okay, well, I am going to find him and make sure he is arrested. No one is going to take away my child, do you understand that?"

Mick found he was holding his breath at the sheer ludicrous magnificence of what he'd just heard. It tickled something inside him, whirling around like a feather. "Yes, I do."

"Good. Please don't tell me I'm silly or crazy

for trying it and most of all, don't tell me to leave it to the police."

"Okay."

"Anyway, I am going to the Pick and Pack to find out who that person was who bought the bag full of snack cakes because it seems like that might be a lead."

"You figure they'll tell you?"

"I have a source."

Her chin was up, mouth in a determined line that made her look all of about eighteen. He hid a smile. "Fair enough. I'll try not to cramp your style by following too close."

"You're not going to try to talk me out of it, or order me to go home?"

"No, ma'am. Not my place, and you told me bossing wasn't polite."

"Well, it isn't." She sighed, brushing a speck of something off the dashboard. "Look. I'm sort of a direct type, so I'm just going to say it. I know you feel guilty about my sister's murder. You blame yourself. I did, too, for a while, and maybe part of me still does judging by the way I blasted you at Aunt Viv's, but Tucker is the one who killed her. You don't need to trail around as my personal bodyguard. This isn't your responsibility anymore."

He shifted a fraction on the seat. "I appreciate that."

"And I'd really rather that you didn't. I've got police all over the place, and they don't seem to like you or Mr. Donaldson very much." She took a breath. "You make things harder for me."

"Can't leave."

She cocked her head, a strand of hair falling across her cheek. "Why not?"

Mick looked away at the ribbons of cloud floating across the moon. "I used to have this sense, back in Iraq, a sort of twinge that started up in my gut. Sometimes it was as if I could feel the bad guys coming." He slid his gaze back to her. "Got that feeling now. Can't walk away."

"I don't want to be cruel, but your sixth sense didn't kick in about Tucker."

He wondered if she knew that it was a knife he had twisted deep in his own gut many times over. A breeze toyed with the collar of her jacket.

"You're going to follow me anyway, aren't you?"

He nodded.

"Fine. I'm to going to get some bags of flour while I'm at the Pick and Pack," she said over her shoulder as she got out of the car. "They've got a sale, and I think best when I bake bread, and if I'm going to find Tucker before he finds me, I'm going to need to do a lot of thinking."

Her small silhouette looked slight against the darkness. In a moment, she'd revved the motor and taken off. As he followed, he tried to understand Keeley Stevens. Could the woman think she would be able to find Tucker and have him arrested all by herself with no skills, no training, nothing but a passion to succeed? He smiled in the darkness and thought of his mother. She approached every situation with confidence, never imagining that failure was an option. His father still had the crooked pots from her ceramics phase.

He recalled the day the dog had torn apart Cowboy Pete, his favorite toy. His mother had gamely rounded up a sewing kit, and though she'd never put thread to needle, she reconstructed Cowboy Pete's body. His missing eye was another matter, solved when she'd found a bead from one of her necklaces and glued it in the hapless cowboy's empty socket. Cowboy Pete had never quite looked the same. Funny how Mick counted that raggedy mess of a toy as one of the finest possessions he'd ever owned.

He wondered if Mr. Moo Moo's eye was still safe in Keeley's pocket.

The drive to the Pick and Pack was easy, and they made the trip in less than fifteen minutes due to Keeley's blistering pace. A sprinkling of rain began to fall. The parking lot was fairly empty, only a few cars and a lone attendant rounding up shopping carts. No sign of a motorcycle, but he didn't fool himself. Tucker had managed to find out where Keeley lived and tracked her into the woods, then lured her to a rooftop. He could be anywhere. He jogged from his truck to catch up to her as they entered the grocery store.

Keeley seemed to have a plan. She marched

straight up to the long-haired teen at the register. The kid gave her a frightened double take. "What do you want?"

"What do people usually want at a grocery store, Stephano?" she said, sweetly. "I'm here for groceries, flour, to be specific, but you're going to give me a piece of information, too, because you're a helpful kind of guy."

He chewed his lip. "What kind of information?"

"Somebody came in last night, just before midnight. That's your shift, isn't it?"

He grunted, which Mick could not identify as affirmative or negative. Would it kill this generation to say "yes, sir" and "yes, ma'am"?

"So during your shift, somebody came in and bought a whole bag of nothing but snack cakes. You know the kind with the yellow cake and white creamy stuff inside?"

He lifted a careless shoulder. "I don't remember."

"I think you do, and what's more," she said as she pointed to the security camera, "I think you could let me see a peek at that security tape, couldn't you?"

"No way. I'd get fired," he said, sending a quick look around the store, probably to be sure his supervisor wasn't watching.

Keeley leaned in, looking like a falcon going for the rabbit. "You'd get in worse trouble if I told your parents that you spray painted my shed." She held up a palm. "You can deny it if you want to, but I've got a sweet camera with a zoom lens and boy, did I get a great shot of you two at work."

The kid turned a greenish tint. He scanned the store again. "My boss is taking a nap in the back. You can go in the security room quick. No more than five minutes, hear me?"

Keeley nodded and sauntered away.

Mick gave the kid a grin. "Good man knows when he's beaten, son. I'd give up the spray painting if I were you."

He heard Stephano swearing softly. Chuckling, Mick joined Keeley, who had already plucked the tape from the day before from the shelf and stuck it in the machine, pressing the fast-forward button with an impatient finger.

"That was impressive back there," Mick said. "Why didn't you show his parents the photo earlier?"

She laughed. "I was a stinker of a teen once, too. I was grounded for an entire summer my sophomore year."

"What did you do?"

"You don't have a high-enough security clearance to know that."

He smiled.

She pointed to the time unspooling under the black-and-white video. "We're coming up on it now."

He leaned close, her hair tickling his chin, the strands softer than the down of a baby bird. A lady appeared on the screen, tall with long dark hair loose around her shoulders, maybe in her late twenties. Her mouth was thin lipped, eyes dark and she wore a T-shirt a couple of sizes too big. She said something to Stephano and he answered back, which caused the woman to smile while he rang up her purchase, a dozen snack cakes and two bottles of water. Keeley paused the video and Mick used his cell phone to take a picture of the screen.

Mick heard the sound of heavy feet approaching. "Company." He quickly ejected the tape and returned it to the shelf. They made it through the door just as a man appeared around the corner.

The whip-thin manager in a rumpled white shirt and tie jerked in alarm. "What are you doing back here?"

Mick propelled Keeley around him out the door. "Wrong turn."

Stephano appeared, weight shifting from foot to foot. "I told you, the bathroom's on that side of the store." He jerked a thumb, swallowing so hard Mick could see his Adam's apple bob up and down.

The manager frowned and started to speak when a plaintive voice called from the checkout line. "Can someone help me? I need to buy these diapers, and…"

There was a crash. "Oh, sorry," the voice called.

Stephano groaned. "I think her kid just knocked over the soup-can display. Took me an hour to set that thing up." He turned back to the register, and his supervisor followed.

Mick puffed out a breath. "Soup-can kid has impeccable timing."

"Sure does. We had just enough time to get a picture. I'm going to press Stephano and see if he can tell me what they talked about."

He took her elbow. "I think the next time we show up at the checkout line, we'd better have a bag of flour."

Biting back impatience, Keeley led the way to the baking aisle and selected the flour. She held two bags of flour and, though she did not ask him to, Mick grabbed the other two.

"That's a lot of flour," he said.

"I bake a lot of bread." She also grabbed a box of raisins that was marked down. It felt odd to have a man escorting her through the checkout, strangely domestic, as if they were some normal couple out running an errand. No one would suspect the fear that swirled around her and the guilt that enveloped him. Still, it made her feel the tiniest bit better to know that she wasn't alone, at least momentarily, in this crazy escapade that made her stomach tie itself in knots. Undoubtedly she would be better off without Mick around, but that couldn't be helped at the moment.

It's all for Junie, she told herself. *You can do anything for Junie.*

They waited patiently for their turn at the register. The manager flicked them suspicious glances as he restacked the cans of soup.

"You talked with the snack-cake woman," Keeley said through a smile. "What did you say?"

"Can't remember," Stephano grunted, shoving the bags of flour into paper sacks.

Mick spoke softly. "If you can't remember for us, I'm sure you could recall it for the cops. My guess is they already know your name, don't they, Stephano?"

"Okay, okay," he whispered. "She was pretty, a little bit flirty so I asked her name."

"And?" Keeley said.

"Ginny," he whispered. "That's all I know. Then she left and I never saw her again."

Ginny. They had a name and a face. It wasn't enough, not even close, but it was a start, and Keeley felt some small triumph in it.

As he gathered up the grocery sacks, Mick leaned forward and spoke to Stephano. "Pull up your pants, son, and buy a belt, for crying out loud."

Keeley managed to repress a giggle.

At her house he carried the bags of flour inside and deposited them on the kitchen table. She lugged out her ancient bread machine and set to work mixing flour, yeast, water and salt. The familiar movements soothed her, the soft clicks and whirrs of the blade mixing the ingredients after she plugged it in. It still amazed her that with only a few ingredients and the help of her machine, Keeley Stevens, worst cook in America, could produce a passable loaf of bread.

Mick watched, thumbs hooked in his pockets, shifting his weight from foot to foot. He eyed the corner of the machine, which she had repaired with duct tape after it wobbled its way off the kitchen counter a week before.

"I didn't know how else to fix it," she said in answer to his unasked question.

"No criticism here. I fixed a leak in our rowboat with some duct tape one time."

She closed the lid and put the machine in the sink. "So it doesn't walk off the counter. In another three hours, we'll have bread."

"We? I, uh, I thought maybe you wanted me to go."

She brushed off her hands and sat at the kitchen table. "It occurred to me on the drive over that I don't know how to proceed."

"We're not talking about bread anymore, right?" he said.

"The investigation. Now that I've got a name and photo, what should I do next?"

"My first pass would be to call Reggie and see what he can find out."

"I thought you were angry with him."

"He did a bonehead thing, but he's still my partner in all of this."

She gestured to the chair opposite. He sat and made the call, putting it on speakerphone.

"That's it? That's all you got?" Reggie said.

"That's it," Mick confirmed. "Ginny's her name, and I just texted you the photo."

"Not much to go on. What am I supposed to do with that?"

"Do what you can. I'll do the same."

Reggie paused. "I think we're getting off track here. Tucker's the bad guy. Even if he found a little friend to share snack cakes with, he's still the target."

Mick drummed fingers on the table. "Other angle we can take is the rooftop diagram."

"Where will we get with that?"

"Dunno, but Tucker had some reason for being interested in it."

"Do whatever you want, but I think you're spinning your wheels," Reggie said.

Keeley could hear exhaustion in his voice.

"I'm going to monitor the police radio," he said. "They might stop him at a roadblock. In the meantime, I've got feelers out with some of my buddies, ears to the ground, that sort of thing. When he pops up, I'll get him."

Keeley wasn't so sure. He'd eluded police for months already.

"Hey, uh," Reggie started. "Listen. Um, Keeley, I apologize for putting you at risk today. I saw Tucker there and I forgot about anything but taking him out. It was wrong and it won't happen again."

"Your motives were good," Keeley said. "No harm done."

"Aww, my motives are rarely good," he said with a laugh. "Just ask Mick." Reggie yawned. "I've got to get some sleep. Talk to you mañana."

"Good night, Reg," Mick said.

"Not until Tucker's caught." He disconnected.

"He doesn't sound like he's going to follow the Ginny lead," Keeley said. "Are you sure he's on our side?"

"He's on his side, which happens to be our side because we both want Tucker captured, only…"

"Only what?"

"Reggie would be fine if Tucker wasn't taken alive."

She felt a chill at hearing it spoken aloud. "He wants Tucker dead."

"Don't you?"

The notion surprised her. "I never thought of it. I always wanted him in prison, far away from Junie, and I wanted him to pay for the rest of his life for taking LeeAnn's, but I don't wish him dead."

His brow furrowed. "Why not?"

Why not? Why shouldn't she want the man to die who'd taken her sister's life? The grief and anger pooled inside as she thought about LeeAnn and how much she'd lost. Life was unfair—tragically, hopelessly unfair. "Because I don't want my heart so filled with hate there's no room for anything else."

Mick examined her face as if he was reading the pages of a book. His brown eyes were soft and searching, tender pools in a mountain of a man.

"Your sister would have been proud of you, I think."

She was dismayed to find that his words triggered tears that she quickly blinked away, and went for her camera. "I have to go take pictures."

"Now?"

"I didn't get the shot of the great horned owl, remember? I'm actually getting paid for delivering pictures of raptors in action, and if you don't meet your deadline, well, they don't call back, you know?"

"Yes, ma'am." He stood. "Let's go."

"I can…"

"Go yourself and you don't want me mucking up your shot, yes, I know."

"But you're coming anyway?"

He answered with a shrug.

"Seriously," she said. "If you're going to follow me everywhere, can you at least string some sentences together and stop calling me ma'am?"

He considered. "I'm familiar with bird photography. If you ever want some amazing bald eagle pictures, our Hudson Raptor Sanctuary is the place to go."

"Wow. Two full sentences. That must have taken

a lot out of you." She admired the note of pride that had crept into his voice. "Can you stay out of my way tonight?"

He nodded, and she frowned. "Sorry. I meant to answer with 'I will endeavor to do that, ma'am.'" He gave her a mock salute.

"I'll get my jacket." She went to the back bedroom. Though she wanted to tell him no, to have him depart and leave her raw emotions to heal, she wasn't eager to go prowling around in the dark, and the aggravating, silent man was the only way she would get her pictures tonight. The feel of Tucker's knife at her throat made her shiver. *I want what's mine.* "For Junie, just until we catch him," she told herself.

Her little bedroom was cold, always prone to drafts that required several tatty blankets to offset and still left her needing to wear woolly socks at night. Funny how when Junie stayed over, they snuggled together and the chill didn't seem to bother them. With a sigh, she moved to close the heavy curtains that muffled the cold. It took her a moment to realize the shadow looming in the glass was not from her own approach. Keeley screamed. The gleam of light from a pair of eyes shone in the darkness.

SEVEN

Mick heard a cry from Keeley and he was in motion, sprinting down the hallway, arriving just as something punched through the glass with a loud crack. He had no time to do anything other than put his body between hers and the window in case something else was going to follow. Shards of glass rained down on the flooring. The bottle projectile broke, the flaming rag inside ignited the gasoline with which the bottle had been filled. Flames spilled across the flooring, heading for pillows stacked in the corner.

He shoved her to the door. "Get the fire extinguisher from the kitchen."

Despite the shock, she did not hesitate, pounding away down the hall. He kicked the pillows far from the approaching flames, coughing against the acrid gasoline fumes. Pulling the blankets off the bed, he tossed them away.

The fumes stung his eyes, flames undulating like predators looking for something to devour.

Keeley returned, thrust the extinguisher at him, and he tried to douse the fire. At first the flames resisted, but Mick had decided this fire was not going to win. He stubbornly went at it, approaching so closely the flames singed the tips of his boots and his face felt like a well-done fillet.

Finally, the fire relented. When it was down to a bare flicker he shoved the extinguisher back at Keeley. "Stay here and keep watch."

She nodded, eyes enormous.

"You okay?" he could not stop himself from adding.

"Uh-huh," she breathed.

"Call for help." He made for the front of the house. No cars, no motorcycles. Staying low, he stuck to the shadows, moving as quickly as he could to the back. The backyard was nothing more than a small patch of grass enclosed by a wood fence that had seen better days. A few of the boards had been kicked in. Easy access. The yard had a gnarled apple tree, a small patch that was probably the beginnings of a vegetable garden and an old camper with two flat tires, parked on a section of gravel.

Heart thumping he stayed still and waited. No sound. No whisper of feet in the grass.

"Are you waiting out there, Tucker? Be a man and come out of the shadows," he murmured. He did a slow sweep of the yard, first visually then step by step. Taking a penlight from his pocket, he eased up along the side of the camper. It was the only place Tucker could be if he'd had the nerve to stick around.

Back pressed flat against the cold metal siding, he crept up to the door, ready to test the handle. Slowly, he pulled the latch. The hinges creaked. Either Keeley left it unlocked, or…

Without warning, the door shot open, knocking him on his back on the gravel. He saw the incoming foot just in time to throw up a shielding arm. The kick jarred his forearm and glanced off the side of his head, sending an explosion of pain through his skull.

"Stop," Keeley screamed from across the yard.

Mick rolled over and got to his feet. By the time he made it to the fence, it was too late, as his attacker squeezed through the gap in the fence. He bit back the disappointment that cut at him. *Too slow, Mick. Again.*

"Was it Tucker?" Keeley asked, face milk white.

"Probably. He's gone." Mick rounded on her. "What happened to staying inside?"

"The fire is out. My cell is dead, so I had to call from the kitchen phone. Besides, I figured two of us had a better chance against Tucker than one."

He sighed. "We're striking out so far."

"But I'm armed this time." She raised a frying pan to the light.

In spite of the tension roiling in his gut, he laughed. "Good to know."

The sound of sirens broke the silence. They

trudged back to the house, and Mick checked once again to be sure the fire was completely out.

The arriving police swept the yard, just as Mick had done. They found no trace of either Tucker or anyone else. Nonetheless, the officers took extensive photos and dusted for fingerprints.

"Plenty of prints," Mason said. "We'll see if any of them are Rivendale's."

There was the slam of a car door and John Bender ran in. "I was working late at the office, and I heard the sirens."

Uttley gave him a cursory update.

"I knew he must have come here," John said. "What happened?"

Keeley chewed her lip. "He threw a Molotov cocktail through the window and ran away."

John shook his head. "Please come stay with me. I can't stand worrying about you every minute. I know you don't sleep well as it is."

Mick saw color flame into Keeley's cheeks. "LeeAnn was the insomniac. I sleep just fine."

John must have seen it, too. "I have a spare room," he said defiantly. "It's not safe to stay here alone."

"We'll put an officer outside," Uttley said.

"Should have been here already," John snapped. "Why wasn't anyone watching her?"

Uttley fixed steely eyes on John. "Because, Dr. Bender, this is a small department and we've already increased the patrols in the area. The officers have other duties, too. I've got to arrange for some off duty people to come back in and bring in some mutual aid." His glance shifted to Mick. "Plus it seems she's got someone watching her back already."

Mick didn't like the look, nor the tone. "Happened to be here, but like you've reminded me, I'm not a cop. She needs police protection."

"She needs to come stay with me," John said. "I'll make sure nothing happens to her. LeeAnn would want it that way."

"How do you know what LeeAnn would have wanted?" Mick could not believe he'd said it, actually used her name out loud, but there was no turning back the anger that ticked up inside. What did this scrawny neighbor know about anything?

John's chin went up. "Because she loved me."

In your dreams. Mick caught himself before he said it aloud.

"It's not your call, Dr. Bender," Uttley said.

His chin went up. "I'll do whatever I have to do to keep Keeley away from Rivendale."

"Enough." Keeley shouted the word that stopped all three men in midsyllable. She fired a withering glance at them. "I am not leaving this house. I am going to do whatever I can to help capture Tucker so I can have my life back. Whoever wants to play bodyguard can jolly well pitch a tent in the front yard, but Tucker took away my sister and separated me from Junie and I'm not, let me say it again, *not* going to let him drive me out of this house."

Uttley blinked. Mick stilled the smile that threatened. Tough as steel. Lovely as a sunrise. Keeley Stevens continued to surprise him.

"I'm trying to keep you safe," John said, taking hold of her forearms.

Mick itched to move him forcibly out the front door.

"Thank you," she said. "But it's not your job to keep me safe." She added in a lower tone, one filled with compassion. "And it wasn't your job to protect LeeAnn, either."

No, Mick thought with a sudden stab of pain. *It was mine.*

John fell back a step, breathing hard through his nose. Without another word he turned on his heel and left.

Mick didn't mind that one little bit.

The police finally departed. Keeley felt the fiery courage that had filled her only a few moments earlier ebbing away. She caught sight of her precious camera and groaned. "And I still didn't get my picture."

A beeping noise sounded from the kitchen, but she could not move from the sofa where she had collapsed.

After a moment's hesitation, Mick snapped into action. With a pot holder, he removed the browned loaf of bread from the machine and set it on the counter, whacking it gently loose from the pan.

"Butter's in the fridge," she said automatically.

"Do you want a slice now?" he said.

"Yes. With butter, please. Lots."

He duly slathered a slice for her and carried it to her on a piece of paper towel.

"You eat a piece, too," she said.

"Not…"

"Please."

He cut another slice, sans butter.

They ate.

The warm, tender bread, studded with cinnamon and raisins and glistening with melted butter settled her nerves. "Do you like it?"

He gave her a thumbs-up.

For some reason it pleased her to know it. "It makes the best toast in the morning. Junie loves raisin toast." A rush of grief surged through her body, and it took every ounce of self-control for her not to cry again. "I want my baby back."

"Good news is Tucker doesn't know where she is, or he wouldn't have bothered busting your window."

She stared at him. "You sure know how to cheer a girl up."

He sighed. "Sorry. I could try to help."

"How?"

"Tomorrow, I can drive you up to our sanctuary. You can get some amazing photos there, I promise."

"And?"

"And what?"

"I hear an ulterior motive in your voice."

"And my father's a retired private investigator. He might be able to help us get a lead on Ginny."

She examined him closely. Broad shoulders, fingers drumming on the knees of his jeans, square jaw tight with some kind of tension. "What I really want is to do this alone, Mick. I know you're trying to help, but having you here, it's hard for me."

He did not look away, merely accepting. "I understand."

"But I will do what it takes for Junie, and if your father can help, then I'll go see him."

He nodded, and she could see neither relief nor satisfaction in his eyes, only a flat, wide expanse of darkness, like a long stretch of bad road. She sensed it had been a torturous journey for him since LeeAnn died, too. That was something they had in common.

He got up. "Got any duct tape left?"

"Why? Is the bread machine letting loose?"

"For the window."

The window, of course. It was now smashed, her room smelling of gasoline. She fetched some cardboard and tape, and while Mick patched over it, she cleaned up the glass and fire extinguisher powder. The room still stank, so it would be the couch for her tonight.

Was Mick going to make the long drive back to the sanctuary? Or stay with his friend Reggie? She wondered why she cared. He was so closed off.

He answered her question later, as he returned the tape to the kitchen drawer. "An hour and a half to the Sanctuary. Best birding is in the morning. Leave at 5:00 a.m.?"

If he expected her to flinch at the time, she wasn't going to give him the satisfaction. She checked her watch. "Sure. It's only eleven. That will give me a whole six hours of sleep."

"You need more than that?"

He wasn't joking, as far as she could tell. "No," she said. "Where are you going to get your six hours?"

"Don't need six. Gonna sleep in the truck, since I didn't bring my tent."

A glimmer in his eyes revealed a hint of humor there.

"Why don't you stay in the camper out back?" she heard herself saying.

"Appreciate that," he said, straightening as if he was standing at attention. "The truck's adequate."

And you don't want to take anything from me, more than you already have. Good, she thought, *because I don't have anything to give you.*

He closed the door behind himself and she locked it. Then she rolled into a ball on the couch, covered herself with as many blankets as she could and prayed.

* * *

It hardly seemed like six hours before her phone alarm beeped. She staggered into the kitchen and started the coffeepot. While it perked she threw on some clothes. The house was dead quiet. Mick must have not woken up. It gave her some small satisfaction to realize the guy was not as iron tough as he seemed.

Until she looked out the front window and saw him sitting on the front step, ramrod straight, long arms perched on his knees. How extremely awkward. After several minutes of wrangling, she finally yanked open the door. "Well, come in already, I've got toast, and don't try to tell me you aren't hungry."

He followed her inside and sat stiffly at the kitchen table. He accepted two slices of raisin toast without butter and a cup of coffee, which he appeared to be trying to sip yet managed to down in three swallows. She refilled it, examining him. His face was scratched, but he didn't appear to be as tired as she felt. There was no dark shadow of stubble across his chin. How had the man possibly managed a shave?

"You can call her from the road," he said.

Keeley plunked her mug down so abruptly the coffee sloshed out. "What?"

"Call the child."

"Her name is June. How in the world did you know that's what I was thinking?"

"You've checked the clock three times since I sat down. And that's what a parent would do, I gather."

She huffed out a breath. "Sometimes I still can't wrap my mind around the fact that I actually am a parent."

His smile was sad. Wistful?

Something unexpected stirred in her mind. "Mick, do you have kids?"

The mug looked small in his big hand. The silence drew on for what seemed like a very long time. "No," he finally answered. "I don't."

EIGHT

Mick briefed the on duty cop as they pulled out. The guy was not pleased at their travel plans, but he'd just have to deal with that. Hunkering down hadn't accomplished much. If it was going to be a fight, Keeley seemed intent on making it a battle of maneuver instead of a battle of encounter. She had some of the qualities of a fine marine, he thought.

Mick had already laid things out for Reggie the night before.

"You should stay put and get yourself a weapon, but I'm sure you're not going to do either of those things," Reggie had huffed.

Mick felt uneasy about the drive. It was not so much that Tucker was possibly tracking their every move, as the fact that he knew Keeley was not the type to be able to sit silently for the duration of the trip. She would talk and she would expect him to reciprocate. There would be sharing involved. The thought made him sweat. Talking was like the embroidery his mother used to try to teach him before she died, all delicate strings that knotted and bunched against his clumsy efforts.

He'd never been much of a talker, but LeeAnn's murder left him even more taciturn, which probably explained why his girlfriend of four months has finally dumped him six months ago.

"You're a prisoner," Beth had said the last time she'd seen him. "You let Tucker escape, and you stepped into the cell yourself."

At the time, standing there in the exhaust fumes from her departing car, he'd berated himself for telling her about Tucker in the first place. See where sharing had gotten him, but her words prickled back through his mind. A prisoner of his mistakes.

You can't outrun shame. His grandfather would have added, *Only God can take it away, Mickey. Only God.*

Yeah, well, Mick wasn't about to go down that road. A man shouldered his own burdens, and he wouldn't ask anyone, especially God, to relieve him of a burden he deserved completely. He wasn't running after absolution. He didn't deserve it anyway.

With his game face on, he opened the passenger door for Keeley. She stared quizzically for a moment.

"Oh. Thank you. No one has done that for a long time. It's nice." Her cheeks reddened and he swallowed hard as she climbed onto the worn front seat.

Did she think he was trying to play the part of a suitor? No, she would surely not have thought that.

Had she? Great. He hadn't even opened his mouth yet and already he was confused. He got in and they drove up the highway. The silence lasted for a good half hour until he felt her looking at him.

He kept his eyes on the road.

Her gaze bored into him still.

"What?"

"You drive slowly."

He checked the speed gauge. "Fifty-five. It's what the sign says."

"Nobody follows that rule."

"Almost nobody."

She laughed, and it was a delicate sound, musical. He was glad he had somehow caused it to happen, though he didn't see the humor.

"Don't marines value speediness?"

"Not if it gets you dead. Slow means I can avoid all the nuts on the road."

"Hmm. I think that might include me, because I'd be doing sixty-five here, easy, unless I had Junie in the car."

He saw her clutch the phone tighter and he knew she was resisting the urge to call. *Gotta wait until sunrise*, he could imagine her saying to herself. Too early to wake the child and her aunt.

After another fifteen miles, her attention was caught by a small roadside garage with a cracked sign tacked to the front.

"Quick Stop Garage," Keeley said, pointing. "Know it?"

"I don't, but it was the logo on Ginny's shirt when she bought all the snack cakes."

He goggled at her. "You remembered that from the security camera footage?"

"I notice clothes," she said, eyes still riveted out the window. "You can check your cell phone picture if you like. Black lettering on a light-colored background. Quick Stop Garage."

He didn't check. Instead he pulled into the minuscule parking lot, home to a car up on blocks and an ice machine that no longer dispensed anything but rust.

"You…" He was issuing a command to no one. She was already out of the car.

He hastened to join her. It was not yet 6:00 a.m. and the windows were dark.

Keeley rattled the front knob.

"They don't open for another half hour," he pointed out.

She peered in through the window as if she hadn't heard him. "Place is pretty empty. It doesn't look as if they're doing very good business."

He had to agree. The front window was cracked, the front step chipped. Whatever had been growing long ago in the front planter box was now browned rubble, overtaken by a scalp of wild grass. They weren't doing a whole lot to attract customers.

"There's a door around back. I'm going to check," she said.

She trotted off on some detective mission. He

sighed. Trespassing was never a good idea. He just hoped there wasn't a dog. Dogs were a marine's best friend, if you happened to be their handler. Otherwise, you might just look an awful lot like a threat. He still remembered getting on the bad side of a Belgian Malinois after some friendly rough-housing with his handler. A neat row of scars on his lower arm bore witness to that.

As he started to follow her around the corner, he heard the deep growl from behind him.

Figured.

Sighing, he turned and looked down. Way down.

A raggedy terrier no higher than Mick's shin watched him, black eyes bright, one ear flopped over.

Mick made himself smaller, extending a hand to be sniffed.

"Hello. You're not much of a guard dog, are you?"

The creature gave the question a moment of thought before he trotted up to Mick, sniffed his hand and promptly rolled onto his back for a scratch, legs scrabbling in the air. Mick complied, wondering if there was anyone alive who could deny a dog a good belly scratch. He was pleased to see the dog was nicely filled out, and, groom-ing aside, somewhat taken care of. He basked in Mick's patient scratching.

"What's your name, fella?"

"His name is Boots," a voice said, and Mick turned in time to see a shovel arcing toward his head.

Keeley rubbed at the small glass window on the back door, but it did not do much good. The haze made it impossible to see inside. She wiggled the handle. Locked, of course. Since she was not about to break in, there was nothing left to do but return to the truck and wait with Mick until opening time.

The stale scent of cigarettes tickled her nose as a man emerged from a large metal storage shed. He was nearly six feet, still shorter than Mick, but broader around the middle, wearing jeans and a stained T-shirt. His black beard curled over the corners of his mouth, at odds with the bald spot on his head.

He didn't say anything, just stared.

Her stomach tightened. "Hello. I was, uh, looking to see if the garage was open."

His lips twitched. "Can't read the closed sign?"

She forced a smile back. "I must have missed it."

"Most people don't miss it." He smiled, a flash of startlingly white teeth. "What do you want? Really?"

"I was looking for someone and I thought she worked here, maybe."

"She?"

Keeley nodded. "A woman. Her name is Ginny."

The smile flickered but did not dim. "This isn't a nice place for women."

Her skin prickled. She inched toward the edge of the step. He didn't move.

"Okay. I'm sorry to have bothered you."

"You didn't bother me. It's nice to see something pretty." Now he did move, slowly, hands in his pockets, smile still on his face, drifting toward her.

"I'm traveling with someone," she blurted out. "A man. He's looking for me. He'll be here in a moment."

The bearded man smiled even wider. "Don't think so. My brother texted me just before I came out."

Her pulse pounded as he finished.

"Said he was gonna go bash a prowler's head in with a shovel." He grinned wider. "This isn't a nice place for prowlers, either."

The panic started up in her belly. Her mind refused to work out a plan as the bearded man stepped closer. The only idea that presented itself through the rush of fear was to kick him and run the moment he laid a hand on her. He didn't, however, just tapped his cell phone on his thigh and watched her, smile in place, easing closer without any hurry.

She scooted away. There was a clear path now toward the woods that backed the property, but the man probably knew every inch of those woods, every pothole and duck blind. He would catch her…

and then what? Blood pounded in her temples. She thought of LeeAnn. Had she felt fear like this before Tucker killed her?

Her body yearned to flee, but she could not bolt until she knew if there was any way she could help Mick.

A moment more of hesitation and she sprinted toward the front, not daring to check and see if the man was pursuing her. She burst around the corner, deafened by a metallic crash.

A lean man with a pitted face and a goatee recoiled from the impact of smashing the shovel into the side of the garage, the space where Mick's head had been a moment before.

Mick flicked a glance in her direction and then hurled himself headfirst into his assailant's stomach.

The impact sent them both tumbling onto the dirt. Mick's arms tensed and flexed as he fought off the blows. Still the skinny guy held on to the shovel, trying to bring it down on Mick's head.

She fumbled for her phone, but what good would 911 do? There were no rocks that she could throw, nothing but dirt and a small dog prancing on anxious feet. The truck. There was a baseball bat in the back. She'd seen it there.

Sweat trickled down Mick's face. The skinny man rolled on top and shoved his arm on Mick's throat, pressing down, trying to crush his windpipe.

"Hold on, Mick," she shouted, running for the

truck. With hands gone ice-cold she snatched up the bat and ran back, wondering if she had the strength and will to bring it down on Mick's attacker.

Just get there, her brain screamed.

She pounded back and found no one.

The dog eyed her as she looked around.

"Where are they?" she snapped.

The terrier made his way through the weeds and down into an irrigation ditch that Keeley had not seen. She waded through the clinging grasses.

Mick had the man on his stomach, hands behind his back. He was breathing hard, face glistening. The shovel was resting a few feet away. She heaved out a breath.

"Are you okay?" she called.

He stiffened. "Behind you!"

She whirled, bat at the ready, to find the bearded man grinning at her as he peered down into the ditch.

"Got the better of Bruce, huh? He's gonna be mad."

"Stay away," she said, readying the bat.

He laughed. "Nice bat, honey," he said, removing a gun from his pocket. "How does it do against bullets?"

NINE

Mick gritted his teeth, tasting blood from one of Bruce's punches.

Bruce groaned and heaved himself to his feet. Mick divided his attention between Bruce and the guy holding the gun on them both.

"Shoot him, Charlie," Bruce said. "Shoot them both."

"Climb up," Charlie said, gesturing to Mick with the gun. Mick did so, taking his time, strategizing escape plans as he went. He had to pass the keys to Keeley so she could get away. He reached slowly for his pocket.

"Uh-uh," Charlie said. "Keep your hands where I can see them."

Mick stopped, Bruce behind him. He wasn't surprised when Bruce aimed a kick at the back of his knee, which sent him sprawling face down in the weeds. He heard Keeley cry out. She dropped the bat and knelt next to him, but Bruce pulled her away.

"Don't touch her," Mick growled, rolling over.

"Or what?" Bruce said. "You're gonna take me out?"

Mick got to his knees. "I did it once. I'll do it again." Time to stir the pot. "You don't know how to fight."

Bruce's mouth tightened in rage. Anger. Good. It made a man sloppy.

"I'll show you what I know," Bruce spat, taking a step toward Mick.

"I'm right here, big shot."

Charlie broke in. "Settle down, Bruce. Let's see what these good people want with us."

"They're trespassers," Bruce growled. "Who cares what they want?"

"Still," Charlie said, looking at Keeley. "Why did you come here? You're looking for a girl, you said. What girl?"

Keeley eyed Mick. "A woman. We found her picture and she was wearing a T-shirt from your garage. We thought she might work here. That's all."

"Who?" Charlie said.

"Her name is Ginny."

Mick caught a quick exchange between brothers. "Know her?"

"No. We gave away a bunch of T-shirts a while back. She must have found one somewhere. Why are you looking for her?" he said. "She done something wrong?"

"No," Keeley said. "Nothing wrong. We think she might have some information."

"About what?"

Mick started to get to his feet, but Charlie waved the gun at him. "Stay on your knees. Information about what?"

What did the brothers know? "Information about a fugitive, Tucker Rivendale. He's wanted for murder."

Charlie was ready for the question this time. His face was stony. "Don't know him. Or her."

"I…" Keeley started to speak but he gave her a warning glance. "I'm sorry we intruded. Can we go now?"

Charlie cocked his head. "Shame for you to rush off." The smile crept over his mouth. "As I said, we don't get pretty girls around too often."

Mick's gut tightened. "If either one of you touch her," he said, "things will get real ugly, real fast."

Charlie stared at him. "Tough talk for a guy on his knees at gunpoint."

Mick jerked his chin at the gun. "That's a .22 and it's clear you haven't been maintaining it. You've probably got powder and bullet wax residue in the chamber. Good chance you're going to have a misfire."

"Good chance I won't."

"Maybe, but your gun hand shakes, too. With the residue and your unsteady grip you won't hit me square the first time and I won't let you get a second shot off."

Charlie grinned. "And you don't think Bruce is

going to hold you down while I shoot you with my unsteady hand, using my dirty gun?"

"I don't think Bruce has the skills," Mick said quietly. "I think Bruce is clear on that by now, aren't you, Bruce?"

He was playing a dangerous game and he knew it, but Keeley was smart and she'd edged closer to the bat while he'd been taunting Bruce. One good swing and she'd take Bruce out, or at least slow him down while Mick dealt with Charlie.

Charlie stared at him, dark eyes shifting in thought. Then he smiled and put the gun back in his pocket. "No need to be inhospitable."

"They're trespassers," Bruce snapped. "We're just gonna let 'em go?"

Charlie shrugged. "We were within our rights to go after them, but I don't want to explain to the cops about why we shot them in cold blood. Cops always get fussy when there are dead bodies to deal with."

Bruce swore and stalked away a few feet, muttering to himself. The dog sniffed at Mick's feet as he stood.

"My brother doesn't like to lose," Charlie said. "You're lucky I didn't let him hurt you bad."

"He wouldn't have," Mick said.

"Cocky. I like that. Just the same, don't come back," Charlie said. "We don't know the girl or her friend Rivendale. You got no business trespassing, like my brother said. Next time I may just shoot as many times as it takes me to kill you."

Mick shrugged. "Point taken. We'll get out of your hair."

He walked toward Keeley, keeping both Charlie and Bruce in his line of sight.

Bruce glared at him with naked hatred.

She took the bat and gave the dog a caress. Her shoulders trembled under Mick's palm as he guided her back to the truck.

They drove off the lot, both brothers staring after them.

Keeley remained silent for a full four minutes. "They were lying."

"Yes."

"About Ginny or Tucker or both?"

"Not sure."

"We should tell the police."

"We can call from my dad's place. Let's get some distance in case they have friends."

"Mick?"

"Yes?"

"What you said about the gun misfiring? Would that really have happened?"

"Not sure. Wasn't that dirty."

"And his unsteady grip?"

"At that range, he'd have hit something."

"Then if Charlie hadn't fallen for your bluff, you would be dead."

"I don't think he'd shoot."

She turned to him, eyes wide, lips taught. "Don't do that again."

He blinked at her, uncertain. "Do what?"

"Don't risk anything for me, do you understand? I don't want you to." Her eyes blazed blue fire. "I don't want to be indebted to you."

"It was the only way out of the situation."

She fisted her hands on her lap. "I don't want anything from you, of all people."

From you, of all people. After what you did. He trained his eyes on the road.

Her voice softened a fraction. "I'm sorry, but I can't lose my independence to you, or anyone else."

But you don't understand, Keeley. I will protect you whether you want it or not. It's the only thing I can do, he thought.

It's the only thing I have left.

She pressed the phone to her ear, wishing she had a private place to make her call. Mick was already too involved in the details of her life, but she did not want to ask him to stop so she could call privately.

She kept remembering him on his knees, staring into the barrel of a gun.

For her?

No, out of some twisted sense of guilt that would get him hurt or worse, if he stuck around. She would not allow it. The idea of seeing him taken down by Charlie's gun left her insides quivering. "Aunt Viv," she said in relief.

"Hey, Keeley. Derek tells me you're taking a day trip. Is that wise? After Tucker nearly burned your house down?"

Again, her aunt had used Chief Uttley's first name. "I'm perfectly safe." Aside from the fact that they had just been menaced by two crazy brothers. It would just kick her worry into overdrive to get into it. "Is the chief there now? I have to talk to him."

Viv giggled. "Actually, he stepped out to get us some coffee. My machine is on the fritz, but I suspect he just prefers the coffee-shop brew anyway. He thinks I make it too weak."

Keeley squashed herself further against the passenger door. "Aunt Viv, are you…seeing the chief?"

Viv sputtered around for the right word. "That makes it sound so furtive. Yes, we're dating. I got to know him after he investigated my car theft." Keeley pictured her aunt blushing a deep crimson. "It wasn't the time then, but lately we've begun to revisit the issue."

Revisit the issue, as if it was a business merger they were discussing. She smiled. "You deserve someone nice." Viv had been through a messy divorce with an alcoholic husband some twenty years before, which had left her financially ruined and physically depleted. Keeley had asked many times how her aunt found the strength to survive it.

"I didn't. It was His strength, not mine," Viv had

said. And Viv had been a rock for Keeley since the moment she'd learned of her sister's murder.

Keeley thought about the chief's strange reaction to their idea about the girl with the snack cakes holing up with Tucker in the newspaper building. Her stomach tightened. What if he had a compelling reason to discredit the information? "Aunt Viv, does Chief Uttley have a daughter by any chance?"

"Daughter? No. No kids. Why do you ask?"

She blew out a breath and chided herself for her rampant suspicion. "No reason. What is on the agenda for today?"

Viv detailed her plans for an indoor picnic and a Play-Doh party. Keeley's spirit sank lower with each moment. "I wish I could be there."

"You will be soon, love, but in the meantime, rest assured we're up to our ears in cops. Safe as a couple of eggs in the nest."

Viv put June on the phone and they spent a lively ten minutes talking about Bubbles the goldfish that Keeley had purchased for June the week before. Bubbles, it seemed, did not want to use the crayon June had deposited in the fishbowl when Viv's back was turned. Keeley could not hold back the giggles as they talked, and disconnected with the promise to buy a friend for Bubbles.

June sounded stuffy to Keeley. She prayed it was not another cold coming on, which usually kicked off an ear infection. They'd been to the ear, nose and throat specialist regularly since June was born.

Maybe it was time to book an appointment. Or should she wait and see if Junie would fight it off herself? LeeAnn would know. Keeley bit her lower lip, mulling over the next of a million decisions that needed to be made for the child.

Mick drove steadily on, and she thought he was not going to speak at all until he cleared his throat some miles later.

"What color are her eyes?"

Keeley jerked. "Junie's? Blue. Why do you ask?"

He shrugged, concealing what was on his mind behind that rigid mask. She had the desperate desire to crack through that impenetrable wall.

"Why, Mick?" She turned to face him. "Why did you want to know?"

He flinched, twitching on the seat. For a moment, she thought he would ignore her question, continuing on in maddening silence. She was about to turn away in aggravation when he spoke.

"Wife stepped out on me when I was deployed, divorced me shortly after I got back. She was pregnant with our child when she left, but I didn't know. Didn't even know I had a son until she called to say he'd died of SIDS eleven months later. I always wondered..." He cleared his throat. "I mean, I always wondered what color his eyes were."

There was such a wealth of sadness on Mick's face that she reached out and touched his hand where it lay on the seat. The fingers were strong and warm under hers. "I'm sorry. That must have been terrible not knowing you had a child until it was too late."

He looked at her hand covering his, but did not move it away. "Yeah," he said softly. "I went to his grave every day for six months after I found out. I didn't cry once. Then out of the blue, I found a dead eaglet one day in the sanctuary. He'd fallen out of his nest." Mick stared at the road.

"And then you cried," she whispered. How horrible that he'd never even had the chance to know he was a father until it was too late.

A ripple of tension went through her when she realized she and her sister had kept the same secret from Tucker. But he'd been a criminal from the start, a criminal who later turned murderer. They'd done it to protect June. They were justified. Tucker did not have the right to know his child.

"If you had known about Junie when Tucker was on parole, would you have told him?" she asked.

His mouth tightened. "I would have suggested to LeeAnn that she tell him."

"But…"

"I'm glad I didn't know."

When they hit a pothole in the road, he returned both hands to the wheel, restoring the distance between them.

She couldn't rid herself of the image of Mick, racked with grief over the death of a tiny life left untasted, wings never unfolded. What kind of father would Mick have been? She had the sneaking suspicion he'd have been a superb one.

The last leg of the drive took them up into the mountains, forested with a thick stand of pine trees. What would have been a brilliant sunrise was colored by a bank of clouds signaling a spring storm that would arrive shortly. She itched to unpack her camera as she spotted a bald eagle cutting through the sky.

"When can we…?"

He laughed. "I'll take you to the lake now and we can talk to dad after. How's that?"

Her nerves tingled with excitement as they took the slope, eventually stopping at a bluff that overlooked a glittering lake below. The trees that fringed the shore were alive with eagles, the air heavily scented with pine and fir.

She flopped belly down on the ground, taking picture after picture, oblivious to anything but the stupendous variety of life unfolding through her lens. When she finally stopped for a moment, she looked up at Mick, who was watching the eagles, a smile of peaceful pleasure on his face.

He was more than a little handsome, she was startled to discover, when he unshuttered his emotions. The brown of his eyes mimicked the rich wood of the pines, and his strong cheekbones emphasized a mouth that looked, at that moment, both tender and prone to good humor as he scanned the glittering expanse.

He realized she was staring at him, and he looked down at his feet. Blushing, she stood and brushed off her jeans. "You were right. This place is amazing for photography."

"My sister could tell you chapter and verse about the eagles, they're her favorite. They grow faster than any other bird in North America. The babies can weigh eight pounds by six weeks of age."

They marveled for a while before driving back to a two-story, well-tended house with a wide front porch. A neat pile of firewood was stacked nearby. Mick held the door as she entered a living room furnished with a Victorian sofa and upholstered chairs. Not what she'd expected.

Perry Hudson wasn't, either. He was smaller than she'd imagined, soft-spoken, his wire-rimmed glasses magnifying the creases around his eyes. He took her hand with a smile in place. "Ms. Stevens," he said. "Mick texted me you were coming."

"Call me Keeley."

He nodded, smile dimming, hand tightening on hers. "I just want to say that I am extremely sorry about what happened to your sister."

She hadn't expected it. A lump formed in her throat as she looked past him to the row of photos on the wall, of Mick and a redhead who must be his sister, Perry and his two children each cradling fuzzy gray eaglets. There was one of Mick in full marine uniform. She knew Perry had known many heartbreaks, including the death of his wife, the abduction of a child on their property, his own son's retreat into a self-made prison. How had this man tried to comfort his own son, as he was attempting to do now with her? It was too much. She squeezed his warm palm and pulled away as gently as she could. "Thank you."

He led them into the kitchen where they sat with glasses of iced tea.

Mick got right down to business. "Dad, we need to talk to you about finding someone, and we don't have much to go on." Mick showed his father the photo of Ginny on his cell phone.

Perry's eyebrows shot up. He looked from the cell phone to his son. "This girl? You're looking for her?"

"Yes." Mick frowned. "Why? Do you know her?"

"Not until two hours ago." Perry crossed the kitchen and called up the stairs. "Would you mind coming down here a minute?"

Keeley tried to process what was going on. She did not have time to do so before the woman from the cell phone picture stepped into the kitchen.

TEN

Mick observed the woman. She was slender, probably in her late twenties, a bit older than she appeared in the picture, with dark eyes dulled by the shadows underneath. Her hair was mussed, pulled back in a messy ponytail and fastened with a rubber band. She wore a thin sweat jacket, inadequate for the stormy spring morning. "Are you Ginny?"

She nodded.

"Got a last name?"

She stared at him. "Ginny's okay for now."

Perry stood and pulled out a chair for her and looked at Mick. "Cooper spotted her about six miles down the mountain when he was on his way up here to get his laptop. She said she was coming here to visit the sanctuary, but her motorbike was out of gas, so Cooper filled the tank for her and brought her up. She seemed exhausted, so I suggested she rest for a while. When I looked in on her she was sound asleep."

"Sorry. I guess I got overtired." Ginny drummed

ragged fingernails on the tabletop. "Haven't had much sleep lately."

"Why were you on your way here?" Mick asked.

Ginny shrugged without looking at him. "I heard about the sanctuary. I wanted to see it."

Mick shook his head. "Try the truth. We know you were recently in the company of Tucker Rivendale."

Keeley stiffened at the name, but kept her lips clamped tightly together.

Ginny turned dark eyes on him now. "So? He's my friend."

Incredible. "He's a fugitive, a killer."

"No," she said, slapping a palm on the table. "He was framed."

Mick almost laughed, torn between bitterness and pity that the girl apparently believed what she said. "Framed? How convenient. And what a coincidence, because just about everyone in prison has been framed for something."

Ginny folded her arms across her chest and fired a look at Mick. "You were his parole officer, weren't you? You knew him better than anyone else and you told the parole board your opinions. Did you think he was capable of killing a woman?"

Fury and shame circled in his mind. He wanted to shout at her but he kept his voice down. "No, I didn't. And I was wrong."

"You weren't," she said. "That's what I came here to tell you. I knew this was your family's place and your dad could get you the message. Tucker is innocent of murder."

Keeley shook her head.

Mick let out a breath. "Okay, I'll play. Just for the sake of argument, if Tucker didn't kill Lee-Ann, how did her body find its way into the trunk of his car?"

The color drained out of Ginny's face. "I can't say."

"Can't or won't?"

Fear sparked in her eyes. "Listen, I came to deliver that message and I did. That's all I'm going to talk about. I didn't expect to see you."

"Or me?" Keeley said. Her face blazed with intense emotion. Mick's heart tripped.

"Do you know who I am?" Keeley demanded.

Ginny's glance flicked to the floor. "The sister."

"Not 'the sister.' I am LeeAnn's sister. Tucker killed her and stuffed her into the trunk of his car like a bag of garbage. I know you want to believe he's innocent because you think you love him or something. Well, you know what? My sister loved him, too, and she believed in him and now she's dead."

"I'm sorry about that, but it wasn't Tucker. I'm telling you."

Keeley leaned forward, her tone pleading. "Listen to me. He's charming, he's charismatic and he's made you believe his lies, but you've got to wake up before you get hurt."

Ginny chewed on her thumbnail, avoiding Keeley's gaze. "Tucker isn't the one who's going to hurt me."

"Did he send you here?" Mick said.

"No. He doesn't know I came. I'm helping him. I have to, after what I've done."

Keeley quirked an eyebrow. "What you've done?"

"If he had guts," Mick said, "he'd have come to me himself."

"Guts?" Ginny glared. "He's been shot at and blackmailed at every turn. Why should he trust you?"

Mick frowned. "Blackmailed? How?"

Ginny's face blanched. "Never mind. He told me you'd never believe a single word that came out of his mouth."

And he's right about that.

"The important thing is he wants to meet his kid…"

Keeley stood, her chair scraping the floor. "Don't say another word. Junie will never be his child. I can't sit here and listen to this." She slammed through the door and outside.

Mick fought the urge to bolt after her.

Ginny stared at the door, which bumped in the wind, creaking on worn hinges that Mick had oiled more times that he could count.

"Ginny, you need to tell me where Tucker is. Where is he staying?"

She shrugged. "I don't know and I wouldn't tell you anyway because you'd hand him right over to the cops."

"Why was he on that rooftop? What's his interest there?"

"I don't know."

"How did you meet him? Did you work at the Quick Stop garage together?"

Her mouth fell open and then she recovered. "I don't know that place."

"Yes, you do. You were wearing a T-shirt with their logo when you bought the snack cakes."

"Maybe I got it at a secondhand store."

"And maybe you didn't." Mick stood, temper rising. "You have to tell me what's going on and where I can find Tucker before he hurts you or Keeley, just like he did to LeeAnn."

Ginny leaped to her feet. "He's not gonna hurt me. He didn't hurt anyone. He's in danger." Tears spilled down her cheeks. "That's all I'm saying. I shouldn't have come here. I don't know what I was thinking. I should have called or sent a letter or something. I always make stupid choices." Her cries turned into full-blown sobs. "I've messed up all the important things in my life."

His anger turned to pity. *Me, too*, he thought. Still, he did not offer comfort. That softness inside him was the reason he'd made the colossal mistake about Tucker in the first place. Instead he retrieved a tissue box from the sideboard and nudged it over to her.

Perry touched her gently on the shoulder. "Let's take a moment to calm down. Son, go look after Keeley while I fix something for Ginny to eat. I can hear her stomach growling. A grilled-cheese sandwich. It's early for lunch, but I'm thinking you probably didn't have breakfast."

"Or dinner last night," Ginny said as she sank down again on the chair, head propped in her hands while Perry fetched bread and cheese. "I haven't been feeling well. I think I might be running a fever."

Mick went outside, sucking in some deep breaths of cool mountain air. A bank of dark clouds ribboned the sky as the morning gave way to noon, the air crisp and clean with the promise of rain. Keeley sat on a rough-hewn log that served as a bench for people waiting to take a tour of the sanctuary. She was hugging herself, cold probably, and he grabbed a blanket from the porch.

She looked up when he draped it over her shoulders. "I guess that wasn't the way to handle an interrogation. I'm not usually prone to outbursts," she said. "I didn't want to hear her say that Tucker was coming for Junie, to defend him as if he was some kind of misunderstood hero."

He sat next to her. "No problem."

"Did you get any information out of her?"

"Not much. My dad is feeding her at the moment." He sighed. "Dad's answer to any crisis is grilled cheese." He recalled the night he'd gotten word about LeeAnn's murder, how he'd sat numb with horror as his father had prepared him a grilled-cheese sandwich. To the present day he still could not stomach eating one. "We'll start up again when she's calmer."

Keeley worried her lower lip between her teeth. Tiny freckles spangled her cheeks against creamy white skin. He had the sudden desire to wrap her in an embrace that would press away the pain, wanting to feel her silken hair against his cheek again, the warmth of her breath on his neck.

You brought the pain, Mick. Remember that.

He cleared his throat. "Do you… Is there anything I can do to help you right now?"

She closed her eyes. "I can't stand it, hearing her talk about Tucker as if he is a good person, as if he has the right to step in and meet his daughter." Tears squeezed through her fringe of lashes. "I want to move on and take care of Junie, but I can't do that until he's out of our lives."

"We'll make it happen." Big words, and he hoped with all his might he could make them come true.

"Sometimes I wonder if he will ever be gone. I mean, even if he's in prison, will he always be on my mind? I pray to let it go, but it seems like we'll never be free of him. I don't understand why God doesn't take this away, do you?"

Though he knew she wasn't really asking him,

he struggled to find something comforting. "I don't ask God for things anymore."

She cocked her head, hair framing her face and such softness in her eyes that it tore him up. "You don't believe in God?"

"I believe, but I won't accept."

"Accept what?"

He didn't want to say it. "Forgiveness."

She reached out her hand and slowly twined her fingers in his, hers small and slender against his calloused ones. "Because you don't think you deserve it?"

He didn't answer, squeezing the satin of her skin, feeling the pulse dancing like a tiny bird where their wrists pressed together. The words wouldn't come, only the feeling of guilt, and shame, and sorrow.

"No one deserves it," Keeley said, voice barely above a whisper. "But if you want it, it's yours. That's what LeeAnn used to say."

He gazed into the blue of her eyes, pools of sky that mirrored his shame back at him. He reached up and traced a finger along the curve of her cheek. She was so lovely, the most breathtaking woman he'd ever seen. "I can't take what I don't deserve," he said.

"That's why it's called grace." She captured his hand and turned it so her lips skimmed his palm. He felt as if his heart expanded so much it was going to erupt through his chest.

He moved closer, his mouth inches from hers. *What are you doing, Mick?*

He got up and headed for the house, the feel of her skin still tingling on his own.

The rain began to fall some thirty minutes later. Keeley clutched her camera, carefully bagged, and started along the path.

Mick hadn't questioned the logic of a picture-taking adventure in inclement weather when she'd gone into the house to retrieve her camera. She suspected he knew that she could not bring herself to stay and listen to Ginny defend Tucker. Perry had informed them that Ginny was lying down on the upstairs bed for a while, pleading a headache. Her shivering indicated she was actually feverish, and Perry administered Tylenol and bundled her with blankets. Mick paced the kitchen, waiting to start the questioning again.

She was grateful, too, to distance herself from Mick. *I can't take what I don't deserve.* While she wanted to classify him as the hardened-cop type who was only a temporary fixture in her life, the hopelessness in his words struck at her. Did he deserve forgiveness for freeing Tucker to kill Lee-Ann? She realized that in her mind he did. The agony in his eyes pleaded for it, even when he couldn't bring himself to ask the Lord. Where there had been anger in her heart before, rage even, toward Mick, there wasn't any. She had forgiven him, and it pained her that he would not accept it from her, nor God.

His choice, Keeley.

But what about Tucker? Was he worthy of forgiveness? Keeley sped up, crunching over the wet pine needles as the path steepened. God could forgive Tucker, but she could not. He had not asked for it, not grieved the terrible choice he'd made, not repented for taking away the sweetest thing in her life.

"He's sorry for how he acted about the pregnancy," LeeAnn had said. "I forgive him, sis. When the time is right, I'm going to tell him about Junie."

But LeeAnn had been wrong, fatally mistaken, and now it was Keeley's job to keep Tucker away from Junie. To keep everyone away and out of their lives. She thought about the gun pointed at Mick, and the feel of his finger tracing her cheek, and her stomach quivered. She did not want him on her conscience, or in her heart.

"Find Tucker and end this," she muttered. "Time to start life again with Junie, just the two of us." She climbed on, up the slope and down a side path that eventually became engulfed by a wild tangle of thorny blackberry bushes. She turned back, finding herself disoriented. Even so, she got several nice shots of kestrels and a red-tailed hawk flitting through the dripping canopy above her. Calculating the fee she might be paid for the photos cheered her. She would provide for June. She must.

Turning around she headed back down the path. The rain increased, thundering down in sheets that soaked her in spite of her windbreaker. She stopped to shelter beneath a tree as the day seemed to turn to night. Chiding herself for not paying closer attention to her route, she pressed herself to continue on a downward sloping path that looked promising.

It led to an embankment, which paralleled a gravel path. Some six feet below, a rushing river of water careened along. She took cover under the spreading boughs of a pine tree, rough bark pressed into her back.

Her stomach twisted into a tight knot as she sheltered her phone with one hand. Should she text Mick? How completely ridiculous that she should become lost in the woods like a child. He would not ridicule her, but she stowed the phone anyway. Best to wait out the rain and follow the gravel path, which she suspected connected to the main road at some point. She'd allow a half hour to orient herself and if no results came of it, she'd swallow her pride and call Mick.

In the distance, through the dripping branches, she noticed a flash of movement. Instinctively, she reached for her camera, ready to capture a deer or bobcat. It was not a raptor she saw through the lens, but a different kind of animal.

And he'd brought along his brother, too.

ELEVEN

Mick finished up his phone call with Reggie, who cut to the chase in his typical fashion.

"Get anything out of the girl?"

"No. She's lying down right now. Sick, she says."

"Uh-huh. And I'm the King of Siam. She's gotta be a diversion. Tucker sent her there with a pack of lies to muddy the waters so he can get closer to his kid. The child is locked down tight?"

"Yeah, Uttley's seeing to that."

"And we trust Uttley?"

Mick hesitated.

"You want me to check on the kid?"

"Appreciate that, but I think we need to work the roof angle."

"I asked. The building is still off-limits until cops are done with their investigation."

"Any timeline on when that will be?"

"Personally, I think they're already done, but they don't want any thrill seekers poking around, or nosy parole officers. I'll inquire again. When are you coming back?"

"We'll wait out a storm and see what we can get from Ginny."

"She's with Tucker. All you're going to get from her is a pack of lies. Best to come back now. Remember, she's learned from the best liar of them all."

The one who fooled you. "Yeah." He clicked off the phone and checked his watch. Ginny was still sleeping. He'd give her another fifteen minutes. Just long enough to go check on Keeley. She wouldn't like it, of course, but there were a million treacherous spots in the woods where someone could go head over heels into a ravine or break their ankle on a log.

"She would call you if she needed you," he said to himself.

He grabbed his jacket anyway, and plunged into the storm. After a mile or two with no sign of her, his phone buzzed.

He read the text from Keeley, gut twisting.

Charlie and Bruce here.

She described her location and he took off at a dead run, feet scrambling for traction against the wet leaves. Near the embankment he slowed, squinting through the rain for any sign of her or the gas station brothers.

"Here," he heard her call.

She was crouched into a ball, back pressed to the tree. He climbed underneath to join her, wiping water from his eyes. He could not resist pulling her into his arms, tucking her head under his chin, just to convince himself she was okay. Her breath warmed his throat and did nothing to restore his calm. Blood rushed wildly through every vessel, muscles craving to pull her closer. Deep breaths. When he could be reasonably sure of his faculties, he let her go. "You okay?"

She nodded, wet hair plastered across her forehead.

"They went that way," she said, jabbing a finger up the slope.

"Heading for the house." He dialed his father's phone.

"Why would they come here?" she said.

There was only one reason: to get Ginny. More than that, he couldn't answer. He pressed the phone to his ear. One ring, two. Five. "Pick up, Dad." It maddened him that his father could never be trusted to charge his phone or have it on him at any given moment. "Not answering. I have to get back there. Going to move fast. I'll double back if you fall behind."

She huffed. "I may get lost easily, but I can run a mile in six minutes flat."

He would have chuckled if he wasn't so worried about what was happening back at the house. "Okay."

Out of nowhere, she kissed him, aiming for the cheek but getting him on the corner of the mouth. Every nerve was electrified by her touch.

He stared at her, skin tingling. "What's that for?"

"For finding me," she said. "I hate being lost."

He nodded, bemused. Just when he was pretty convinced she despised him. Women are a mysterious breed, he thought, not for the first time. "I know a shortcut, but it's rugged."

"So am I," she said.

Yes she was, but soft, too, and warm and enticing, with lips soft as down feathers. Shouldering the thought aside, he hurried toward the top of the slope, along a path that was probably invisible to her eyes. For the past eighteen months, the sanctuary had been his prison and his pleasure; he'd walked every square inch, hiked each forgotten ravine in his effort to understand his own mistakes. Now the effort was put to good use. The slope plunged abruptly downward over a branch of the river that swelled with each moment of the storm. A wide log spanned the creek bed. He offered Keeley a hand, which she did not need, as she crossed nimbly and waited for him on the other side.

Once they climbed from the creek bed it was a two-mile trek. The slope wasn't steep, but rocky enough to slow them down.

"Dad, answer your phone," he said as he dared a

moment to try again. He didn't answer. They took the final mile to the house at a jog. True to Keeley's word, she kept up the pace. He pulled her to a stop near the woodpile. "Wait here."

She shot him a look.

"Bossy, I know, but please. I need you to call the cops."

She started on the call and Mick jogged up the porch steps. The front door was open, the house dark and quiet. He moved forward as silently as he could, avoiding the spots on the wood floor that were prone to squeaking. It was an invaluable advantage to know the terrain when your enemy didn't. He heard the soft creak of the stairs somewhere near the top.

He took them as quietly as he could manage. Halfway up he paused again, listening. There was a shout, a man's, and he threw caution aside and charged up the steps, reaching the door to the room where Ginny was resting just as it slammed shut. Mick threw a shoulder at it. Locked.

He went at it with his boots, furious energy fueling each kick. The solid wood shook beneath his onslaught, and it was only a few minutes before the flimsy lock gave way. He exploded into the room, slipping on the wet floor, grabbing the door frame to keep his footing. The bedroom was empty, water sheeting in through the open window. The bed covers were tousled and half on the floor.

Running to the window, he caught the flicker

of movement from one of the brothers who had climbed down the tall tree just outside the open window. With his knee throbbing from the assault on the door, he figured the faster pursuit would be sprinting back downstairs. He'd just turned to do so when he heard a soft groan coming from the room next door.

Keeley finished her call and crept into the house. Mick was going to need some help dealing with both Charlie and Bruce. Recalling the murderous look on Bruce's face at their last encounter made her skin erupt in goose bumps. She tried the light switch and found it not working. Perhaps the storm had knocked out the power. The rumble of an engine sent her running to the window. She saw Ginny, hair flying, pushing the motorbike to its top speed as she tore out of sight. A second later, two burly figures that she recognized all too well ran back in the direction of the gravel road, likely to find their vehicle and run Ginny down.

"Mick," she yelled. "They're getting away."

"Let them go. She's got a good head start. Get the flashlight in the kitchen drawer, can you please?" he called down. His voice was tense.

Fearing what Mick had found, she tried all the drawers until she found the one with the flashlight and took the stairs two at a time. She discovered them in one of the bedrooms. Mick knelt next to Perry, who lay dazed on the floor, eyes half-open.

Mick took the flashlight and examined his father. "Looks like they hit him from behind. He's got a knot on the back of his head."

Perry groaned and tried to sit up.

Mick restrained him. "Lay still."

Perry cleared his throat and breathed out a puff of air before he spoke. "You're a grown-up, but I'm still your dad, and you don't get to tell me what to do." Perry smiled at Keeley. "He's bossy, isn't he?"

"Yes," she agreed with a shaky laugh. "But maybe we should listen to him this time."

He sat up, pressing a hand to the back of his skull. "Saw them coming and ran for Ginny, but they got me first. Where is she?"

"She must have climbed down the oak tree," Mick said. "Same thing I got grounded for repeatedly as a teen."

"You had it coming," Perry said.

Keeley confirmed that Ginny had made it to her motorbike. "What did they want with her?"

"Whatever it was, it scared her enough to make her bolt. Clearly they're not on the same side." Mick helped his father up and supported him to a chair. Keeley fetched some ice from the kitchen, wrapped it in a towel and gave it to Perry, who pressed it gingerly to his head.

"Somebody called the police?" Perry said.

Keeley nodded. "They're on the way."

He sighed. "Well, while we're waiting, can you

tell me anything about the guys who broke into my house and clobbered me?"

Mick told him as much as they knew about Charlie and Bruce. Perry insisted on moving to a chair in the living room, so Mick hooked an arm under his shoulder and helped him downstairs. He'd just gotten settled when the sheriff arrived, introducing himself as Wallace Pickford. He had a medic check over Perry while Mick went through the story again.

The sheriff's expression darkened. "Going to look at the embankment and make some calls. Be back soon." He excused himself.

Keeley paced the kitchen while he did so, and Mick monitored the medic's examination of his father.

Her anxiety pounded like the storm. Why had the two thugs shown up to snatch Ginny? Or, Keeley thought with a fresh swirl of alarm, had they intended to kill her?

Mick joined her in the kitchen.

"Is your father going to be okay?"

"I think so. Medic says he doesn't suspect a concussion. Dad's too stubborn to go to the hospital. My sister is on her way, so maybe she can talk some sense into him."

"I called home. Viv and Junie are fine. There's an officer with them and no sign of trouble, but Uttley told her he's going to double up the watch."

"That's good."

"But what if Uttley isn't to be trusted?" she blurted out. "Do you believe him?"

He hesitated. "I'm not a good person to ask about that."

"Please," she said, laying a hand on his hard-muscled chest. "I need to know what you think, Mick."

He pursed his lips, silent for a moment, covering her hand with his. "I think there's some other player in this game besides Tucker."

Something cold swept through her veins as she turned away, leaving a trail of panic in its wake. She wanted to run to Junie, sweep her away from everyone and flee, just the two of them. God would sustain them; she knew He would. They didn't need help. Keeley could be enough for Junie.

But looking into Mick's face, she understood that now the game they were playing was one she could not win alone. Was it possible God had brought Mick to her now for that very reason? She needed Mick, and she couldn't restrict his involvement, as much as she wanted to, because there was no other option. A thought tickled her mind. She swallowed. "I don't know what we should do next."

"See what Sheriff Pickford can find out. He's impartial, at least to this investigation."

She nodded. The clock on the mantel chimed three. Had the whole day flown away so fast? The rain beat on the windows and lightning strobed the sky. "Should we drive back?"

"I'd like to stay until my sister arrives, if you don't mind. And I want to hear what Pickford comes up with. Can you stand it?"

Could she? Her nerves clamored to drive back, to be at least in the same city as her child. But what was to be done there? She couldn't see Junie and she, too, needed to know what the sheriff could tell them about the mysterious Ginny and the crazy brothers. Besides, there was something awkward and raw about being here in the home where Mick lived, closeted away from the grief he'd had a hand in causing. She felt a flare of jealousy that he could make such a choice while she had to go on living, day after day, with the aftermath of losing her sister. She'd not had the option to hide away like Mick had.

"Yes," she said, jaw set. "I can stand it."

It was almost an hour before an auburn-haired young woman burst through the door, heading right for the armchair and throwing her arms around Perry. "Are you all right? Who were the guys that hurt you?" She peppered him with questions until he held up a hand.

"Sit down, Ruby," Perry said, "and we'll fill you in."

It seemed though, that Ruby was not capable of sitting. Instead she kissed her brother and traced a finger over a scratch on his face. He gave her a squeeze. "Quit fussing. I'm fine. This is Keeley Stevens," Mick said.

Ruby came near, extending her hand for a solemn handshake. "I'm sorry it's such poor circumstances, but welcome. I'm glad to meet you. I brought some clothes because Mick said you needed some dry ones."

Keeley thanked her, surprised that Mick had thought about her well-being. She noted Ruby's subtle scrutiny, no doubt trying to figure out how the sister of a murdered woman fit into her brother's life.

Don't worry, Keeley wanted to say, *I don't. We're just partners. All business.*

She dutifully followed Ruby to a small room crowded with bunk beds and a tiny dresser where Ruby offered her a selection of clothes. "These sweats are mine, but I'm a little more full figured than you. You can adjust the waist, and here's a sweatshirt and socks and underwear."

Keeley smiled, thinking that her sister LeeAnn would have been just as resourceful in clothing a bedraggled soul. "You are very sweet. I appreciate it."

Ruby smiled. "Oh, I've had more than my share of people taking care of me through the years, especially Mick."

Her dark eyes flicked across Keeley's face. Keeley stayed silent.

"How well do you know my brother?"

There was a wealth of undercurrent in the question. How well did she know Mick Hudson? She discovered that she knew only two things for certain: first, despite his extreme reserve and awkwardness, Mick Hudson was a man of courage. Second, he'd decided to rescue Keeley Stevens, whether she wanted him to or not. "Not well at all," she said.

Ruby sighed. "He doesn't let anyone know him, really, not anymore. Not after…"

"My sister died?"

She nodded. "Yes, but it started earlier, when his wife left him, I think, and other things."

"He told me about his son."

She started. "Really? I'm surprised. He doesn't ever talk about that. He's very gracious about his ex, Denise," Ruby said. "He figures he didn't pay enough attention to her, didn't realize she wanted different things out of life. Me, I'm not so gracious. She cheated on my brother and took his son away. If Liam hadn't died so young, I wonder when she would have gotten around to telling Mick he was a father."

"Does Mick ever talk to her?"

"No. She's moved on with a new life. Mick still goes to the cemetery every month and trims the grass. They have people to do that, of course, but Mick doesn't think they give it the proper marine precision."

Keeley could picture Mick, in his methodical way, tending to his dead son's grave. It made her want to gather him in her arms and keep him close. She busied herself bundling the clothes instead.

Ruby acted as if she wanted to ask another question, but Keeley was relieved when she didn't.

"Anyway, I'll let you change while I check on Dad. I'll make him tea. Personally, I can't stand tea, but I hear it's therapeutic after a shock."

In a flash, Keeley remembered all the well-meaning people in her own life who had offered her tea in the wake of the news about LeeAnn's murder.

She remembered John, white-faced, eyes horror-struck, handing her a steaming mug with trembling hands. "How can we live without her?" he'd whispered.

"I don't know" had been her silent reply. She still asked herself the question every morning and somehow, God gave her the strength to live one day. And then the next. It was only lately that she'd begun to live as if there might be a future in store for her and Junie.

Back then, the one thing those cups of tea had accomplished was forcing her to hold on to something solid when everything else in the world disintegrated around her.

Was the same thing happening now? Was the kindness and peace she'd come to know lately dissolving once more into violence?

Lord, please let me protect Junie.

And, she added, *help Mick to heal.*

TWELVE

Mick was grateful that Ruby kept Keeley busy preparing a pot of soup. It was preventing her from going mad with waiting, he figured, and it freed him from trying to make awkward conversation. He found his gaze returning to the kitchen as she drifted in and out of his line of sight, baggy sweats engulfing her slender legs. His spirit lifted on her delighted tone when she discovered a bread machine in the cupboard. He smiled, thinking about her old broken machine that she'd mended with duct tape. He'd get her a new one, he decided, before he left Silver Creek for good.

"Son?"

Mick realized his father had been speaking to him. "What did you say?"

Perry quirked a lip. "Nothing important. Can you get me my laptop? Let's see what we can find out while we're waiting for the sheriff."

Mick fetched the laptop, caught by the sound

of Keeley's and Ruby's mingled laughter as they peeled carrots and chopped onions.

"You're fond of her, aren't you?"

Mick fumbled the laptop as he handed it over. "Fond? Uh, no. Well, I mean, she's a great woman, but I'm just…" He swallowed. "I'm just helping her out until we find Tucker."

"Until your debt is paid? So this is just about making amends?"

"Dad, I can't make amends. I'm the reason her sister is dead. You can't undo something like that."

Perry ran a thumb over his bottom lip, staring at a wedding picture on the mantel. "You know, Mick, I never really understood your mother. She was a city person who loved her beautiful clothes and fine furniture. She could spend hours in an art gallery or at a concert when I'd be looking for the door in five minutes. I loved her madly, but I never understood her, never could believe her strength. To me, she was a mysterious thing, like the arctic tern. How can a four-ounce bird travel some twenty-five thousand miles in a single migration? Your mother was strong like that, too. Incomprehensibly strong."

Mick listened in silence, hanging on to the words about his mother, who had died from ovarian cancer when he was in grade school.

"Your mom was flighty as a bird, too, but underlying that was a firm and unshakable faith. She would have said guilt is a prison and God puts the key in your hand. All you need to do is take it and let yourself loose."

"But you don't believe that, do you, Dad?"

"I never figured I needed God."

Mick held his breath. He'd learned his faith from his mother, and he knew it was an enormous step for his father to be entertaining thoughts of God.

"But, Mick, I'm beginning to rethink some things."

They let the idea sit there awhile and take root.

"I'm just wondering, son. All these years I've lived apart from God, my sins unforgiven." He locked eyes on Mick. "And you've known God all this time, and yet you believe your sins are unforgiven, too."

"Dad…"

"So which is it? Are you forgiven or not?"

A maelstrom of confusion and emotion left him unable to answer.

Perry put his hand over Mick's. "Maybe we both need to take up that key that your mother talked about."

Mick clasped his father's hand, noting that it was not the same strong palm that he'd known as a boy. The bones and knuckles seemed more delicate now. "I'm confused, Dad."

"Me, too, son. I wish your mother was here, because she'd know what to say, but I know she'd think I'd finally gotten some sense in my thick head. Maybe yours, too. Can we agree to mull it over in that slow-witted way of ours?"

Mick sighed. "Yes, sir."

A knock at the door saved Mick from his distress. He opened the door and readmitted Sheriff Pickford. Ruby and Keeley joined them.

"Your entrance road is under a couple of inches of water right now. If it doesn't let up soon, it won't be passable, so I'm gonna make this quick," the sheriff said, easing his bulk into an armchair. "Who exactly made an identification of these two brothers?"

Keeley leaned forward. "I did. I saw them down there by the embankment."

"What about you?" Pickford said to Perry. "Did you see their faces?"

"No, they hit me from behind."

"What difference does it make?" Mick said. "We know it was them."

Pickford shrugged. "That's the burden of law enforcement. Knowing and proving are two different things."

True enough. It wasn't long ago that their whole town had believed without a doubt that Ruby's now brother-in-law was responsible for the child abducted on their property. He was guilty of the misjudgment himself. Knowing and proving were really two different animals. "We know their names, their place of work, we had an encounter with them earlier, what more do you need for proof?"

"Something to break their alibi would be nice."

"What alibi?" Keeley said.

Pickford rubbed a hand over his stubbled chin. "According to Frank Carter, the owner of the scrap-metal place in Downeyville, Charlie and Bruce were at his shop this morning and stayed there for lunch."

"You've got to be kidding me," Mick snapped.

"Tuna fish on rye," Pickford said, "and some leftover peach pie."

"Carter is lying."

"Probably, but it's your word against theirs."

"I saw them on the sanctuary property," Keeley said. "Doesn't that count?"

"Would count more if you weren't such a distance away in the middle of a downpour. You could have been mistaken."

"I wasn't."

He sighed. "I'm sure you weren't, but we don't have enough to bring them in. That's not to say there won't be an investigation. We've got people out looking for the girl, and Uttley's heading that up."

Uttley. Was he to be trusted? They were back to that question again.

"Can you do any digging about the brothers?" Perry asked.

Pickford's eyes narrowed, sliding to Mick. "That would be stepping on toes. Do you have reason to believe Chief Uttley can't handle the investigation?"

Mick chose his words carefully. "We have a suspicion that Uttley has a connection to Ginny."

"The girl who came here to tell you Tucker Rivendale is not a killer."

Mick saw Keeley flinch. "Yes."

"We've got nothing on her at this point, but I'll tell you what I'll do," Pickford said. "I know a couple of retired cops that used to work for the Big Pines department. I'll give them a call. Unofficially. If I hear of anything that might be helpful, I'll pass it your way."

Mick thanked him. It was the best they could ask for.

He walked the sheriff to the door.

"I'm just gonna say it," Pickford said. "I'm a cop, and cops trust cops. If Uttley is protecting this girl, he's got a good reason, but there's probably nothing to it at all."

Mick thanked him again and closed the door.

Nothing to it at all?

Not likely.

Keeley still stung from the news. Her word wasn't good enough to stand against the alibi of a pair of violent lawbreakers. So much for the justice system. She wanted to get into the truck and go, but Ruby's vegetable soup smelled delectable and Keeley's mouth watered. The morning toast was a distant memory.

The bread machine popped out a perfectly

browned loaf of garlic herb bread that begged to be eaten, so Keeley gave in to Ruby's prompting and agreed they should stay for dinner. There was something comforting and cheerful about gathering around the table with the Hudson family.

Aside from Perry's headache, he seemed to be in good spirits. Keeley enjoyed the easy interplay between the man and his children. It made her miss her own mother, Blanche, who had never quite been the same since LeeAnn's death, either. On the few occasions when Keeley had brought Junie to see her, Blanche remained detached, watching the child as if she was a curious stranger rather than her granddaughter. At least her mom seemed happy in her assisted-living facility, with friends who looked in on her and a cousin just across the hall. Keeley faithfully mailed her a loaf of bread every month.

Perry and Mick both put a slice of Keeley's bread in the bottom of their bowls before ladling the chunky soup over the top. They moved in such unison, she found herself laughing.

Mick looked bemused. "What?"

Ruby grinned. "She's noticing that you two have a strange soup ritual. Cooper has commented, too. He says it's like you eat your soup to get to the soggy prize at the bottom." She checked the time on her phone. "Excuse me for just a minute. I want to catch him while he's on a layover. He would have stayed after he put gas in Ginny's motorbike, but he had to hurry to the airport. He's taking a botany class in New York." She could not hide the rosy glow that crept into her cheeks, nor the pride in her voice. "It's the first time we'll be separated overnight since we got married." She left the table to make the call.

Keeley felt an ache in her heart at Ruby's devotion. How would it feel to commit yourself so completely to a man? Then she considered that LeeAnn had done just the same thing. Keeley shot a look at Mick, contemplating how she'd come to trust him in the past few days, how his cheek felt when she'd kissed him. *Forget it, Keeley.* She would not take the risk of allowing any man close enough to divert her attention from the only thing that mattered: Junie.

Perry tapped his spoon absently on the table. "I've been snooping around on the internet. I still have a few connections at my disposal."

Mick swallowed a spoonful of soup. "Find anything?"

"Nothing recent, but I did some prying into Charlie's and Bruce's pasts."

Keeley could see he'd unearthed something. "What?"

"Bruce has done jail time for minor stuff, petty theft, drunk and disorderly. He bounced around the country for a while until he hooked up with his brother in Texas a few years back. They were under suspicion for a while, but nothing came of it."

Mick folded his napkin. "Under suspicion of what?"

"The cops were cracking down on chop shops."

"Chop shops? Where they take stolen cars?" Keeley asked.

Mick nodded. "It's a very lucrative business. Steal the cars, take them to a garage, where they're stripped for parts and sold. Often they're shipped out of the country, where the rules are less stringent, and it can all be done in hours."

"They did a raid on the brothers' Texas garage one time, but found nothing," Perry said. "They're smart, these brothers, and there's nothing to indicate they've been involved in anything here in Oregon."

"Nothing at all," Mick said softly.

Nothing at all. Keeley took a steadying breath. "Are you thinking what I am, Mick?"

His eyes flicked over her face. "That Tucker went to jail for auto theft?"

"Uh-huh. That seems like a pretty big coincidence, doesn't it? Charlie, Bruce, Tucker and Ginny may all have some connection to Quick Stop Garage. We have to go to Chief Uttley," Keeley said. "He can't ignore this now."

"Agreed. He knows we've filled the sheriff in and that my dad has done some investigating. He won't be able to sweep anything under the rug."

Finally. A solid lead that might take them straight to Tucker.

They continued their meal in relative quiet until Ruby returned. She realized at once that something had changed while she was gone and demanded to be filled in. The revelation seemed to take away her appetite, and Ruby pushed the soup aside. "This is getting too dangerous. I think you two should stay here until it's under control."

"I can't." Keeley balled up her paper napkin. "I have a child to protect."

"Bring her here," Ruby insisted. "We'll watch over her and you."

Keeley saw the earnestness in Ruby's eyes. "Thank you," she said quietly, "but I need to take care of Junie myself."

"You can't do it yourself," Mick said.

Her nerves frayed. "And you can't do it, either."

An awkward silence settled upon them. "I'm sorry," Keeley said. "I'm just rattled by everything that's happened, and I want to go back."

"Of course you do," Ruby said. "I'm not a mother, so I hope you'll forgive me."

Keeley squeezed her hand. *Sometimes I feel as if I'm not a mother, either*, she thought.

An hour after dinner, the storm abated and Mick and Keeley said goodbye to Perry and Ruby. Ruby gave Keeley a hug and did the same for her brother.

"If there's anything…" she said.

"I know, sis."

Ruby smoothed a nonexistent wrinkle from the front of his T-shirt and spoke in a near whisper. "I'll be praying for you—for both of you."

"We could use all the prayers we can get." Mick pressed a kiss to her temple and they departed, easing the truck through the pond that had formed near the entrance gate. They encountered stopped traffic on the main road, due to a car accident.

"Wait or take a longer detour?"

She yawned. "I say the detour."

He looped around and took a mountain road that would get them to the highway eventually. Keeley pulled her jacket around herself. Ruby had insisted on laundering Keeley's soaking clothes so at least they were clean and dry, neatly packed in a paper bag. He flicked on the heater and adjusted the vent in her direction.

She yawned again. "You have a nice family."

"Thank you. They're good people."

"And you're good people, too," she said sleepily.

"Wish my wife had agreed with you." He couldn't believe he'd just uttered those words. What was the matter with him? He fiddled with the heating vent again.

"Your sister talked about her a little."

Great. "She's hard on Denise."

"She thinks you shoulder too much of the blame."

"Oh, man." He sighed. "Fact is, I'm a plain guy. I mean, there are eagles and falcons and such, but

I'm more of a condor. You know, awkward looking, strong. Not the fancy birds that get their pictures on postcards and advertisements."

Keeley cocked her head, the fringe of bangs falling across her forehead. "What's wrong with plain?"

"Denise didn't want that kind of life, and I didn't hear it when she tried to tell me. She didn't want to be a military wife, drive around in a beat-up truck and listen to me go on about birds. She wanted to get her PhD, live in a college town, and I guess she found a guy who wanted that, too. I understand now. I saw her how I wanted her to be, not how she was. My fault, just as much as hers."

"But the baby," Keeley said. "Your son."

"My son," he repeated. The word felt foreign on his tongue, as if he was trying to speak a language he didn't know. "Yeah."

Keeley reached out a hand and laid her palm on his biceps. "I think Liam would have been blessed to have you as a father."

Mick swallowed an ache that crept up his throat. He had not thought of himself as a blessing to anyone for a long time. *Thank you for saying that*, he wanted to tell her, for believing that, but he could not force the words out. Instead he focused on the road, slow and steady, surprised when he felt her body pressed against his side. She'd fallen asleep, lulled by the warmth and probably exhausted by the harrowing days she'd just experienced.

Carefully, he lifted his arm and she folded against him, her head resting on his chest, his arm around her slender shoulders. He breathed in the scent of her as his warmth mingled with hers. For a moment, he allowed himself to imagine what it would be like if Keeley was his, this strong, funny woman with the heart of a lion. They would drive places, take June to see the eagles waking up in the morning, maybe buy her a little fishing pole and teach her how to catch trout. They'd be a family, and he would do everything in his power to make them both happy.

But imagination wasn't going to wash away the past, marked as it was by his part in LeeAnn's death. He shut off his heart to such fantasy and focused.

Drive her home.

Keep her safe until Tucker is found.

Get out of her life.

THIRTEEN

Keeley awoke as they pulled into her driveway, disoriented to find she had been asleep on Mick's shoulder. She jerked upright so fast her vision swam.

"Oh. Sorry, I must have drifted off." She pushed her hair out of her face and her warm cheeks signaled she was blushing madly. "Really sorry."

She saw the glimmer of a small smile.

"Don't be. You were tired. Only got six hours last night."

Her heart still beat erratically. "So why don't you look tired? Never mind. I forgot you don't need sleep."

"I do, just not as much as you."

"What time is it?"

"Almost midnight."

Mick greeted Mason, who walked from his police car to the pickup. "Evening. Have a nice trip?"

Keeley thought *nice* was not the word she'd use for encountering Charlie and Bruce twice and losing Ginny. "We need to talk to Chief Uttley. Can you call him?"

Mason licked his lips. "He got a phone message. Had to take care of some business."

Keeley's heart skipped. "Who's watching Junie?"

He raised a calming hand. "Got two cops assigned there now. They just reported in. All's quiet. Don't worry. Rivendale's not going to come anywhere near her."

Keeley tried to relax. "All right. Can you please tell Chief Uttley we need to talk to him right away?"

"Sure." Mason walked back to his car, a shade too abruptly, she thought.

Mick got out and headed for the passenger door to open it for her, but Keeley hopped out before he got there. Bad enough she was sleeping on the man's shoulder, for goodness' sake. When had she grown so comfortable with Mick Hudson?

He followed her to the door and waited for her to unlock it.

"Mick, you aren't going to sleep in the truck again, are you?"

"Yes, ma'am."

"That's ridiculous. Come inside and sleep on the couch, at least."

"Truck's fine."

She stood in the doorway as the moonlight painted the strong planes of his face. In that light, he did not look anything like an ungainly condor, nor a hard-as-nails marine. Seeing how tenderly he'd treated his father and sister had softened her view of him. She reached out and put a hand on his chest, feeling the strong beat of his heart under her palm. He looked at her hand for a moment, then, slowly, covered her fingers with his.

"Please," she said quietly. "I am grateful that you're here. I don't want to be. I want to take care of it all by myself and be the whole world to Junie without help from anyone, but I can't. I—I need you. Junie and I need you to help us out of this mess."

He traced his fingers, rough and calloused over hers, igniting prickles along her arms.

"That was hard to say," he said, voice low and husky.

"Yes." She blinked back unexpected tears. "I've been very conscientious about shutting people out even when God opens the door and lets them in."

He looked at her then, eyes glimmering pools of deepest shadow. "You have so much courage. More than any soldier I ever met."

She took a deep breath and let go of a portion of her pride. "Will you please sleep in the trailer out back? I would feel so much better knowing you were there in case Tucker comes again, and I don't like to think of you spending the night in your truck." There. She'd said it, thrown out the feeling that had been burgeoning inside her, that small voice that kept insisting that she trust Mick Hudson.

He was silent for so long, she thought he hadn't heard her. Embarrassment pooled in her stomach, and she'd just decided to pull her hand away, go inside and pretend she'd never said it when he grazed her fingertips with his lips and nodded. "All right. Until Tucker's caught."

Relief coursed through her veins. "Good. Thank you."

"I'll check the house before I move my gear to the trailer."

His gear. A mission to complete. Why did it give her a tinge of remorse? *Of course it's a mission, Keeley. For both of us. What else could it be?*

True to his word, he checked every window and door, covering the broken glass with a dry layer of cardboard to replace the one that had gotten soaked in the storm.

"Need to get a new window tomorrow. Easy to install. I can do that for you."

Keeley bit her lip. "Um, actually, the window will need to wait."

He raised an eyebrow. "Not safe to leave it like that."

"I know." She eyed the stack of bills on the sideboard. It would be another two days before the anonymous check would arrive. "It will need to wait a little while."

He took it in, understanding dawning. "Oh. Right."

Cheeks burning once again, she followed him to

the kitchen door and let him out into the backyard. "Okay, then. Good night."

"Good night."

She closed the door. His bulky frame did not move from the porch step. What was he waiting for? She pulled it open again.

"Lock the door," he said. "I mean, could you please lock the door?"

"Yes, sir," she said. "I was intending to." She slid the lock home.

On the way to take the hottest shower she could manage, she checked the message on her phone.

"Hey, Keeley," John said. "I tried calling before, but you weren't answering. Can you help me? I've got the hummingbird almost ready to release, and I did an osprey rescue last night. I'm up to my ears in birds." He laughed. "Anyway, could sure use your help."

She appreciated his tone—not a demand but a humble request. Guiltily she realized she should have been helping him more, especially with the voracious demands of the Anna's hummingbird baby. Quickly she punched in a text. Will be there tomorrow. Sorry.

Should she add something about the past twenty-four hours? How could she capture the crazy actions of Charlie and Bruce? Or her shock at finding out Ginny was already at the Hudsons' house?

Or, she thought, the uncomfortable realization that she had come to trust Mick Hudson.

She left the text the way it was and hit the send button before she took a shower, flopped down on the sofa and slept.

Mick listened to the wind send pine needles dancing over the top of the trailer. It was not yet 4:00 a.m. and he was wide-awake. Though he'd never admit it, the small bed with the musty mattress was more comfortable than his truck, even if his feet hung over the bottom and he had to sleep with his head on the frame. He replayed the moments on the porch step again and again in his mind.

I've been very conscientious about shutting people out even when God opens the door and lets them in.

Was that what had happened? Had God opened a door for him to step into Keeley's life? Cold sweat popped out on his forehead. No, God would not have ushered him into Keeley's life, because if he failed her like he'd done LeeAnn...

Mick sat up. He could not think that way. Keeley was going to escape Tucker Rivendale and Mick was not going to let any odd emotions cloud the issue. Still, he could feel her hand on his heart as she said the words, the press of her lips when he'd found her in the storm.

Junie and I need you to help us out of this mess.

That's it, Mick. They need you for your skills, such as they are, so don't get sloppy. Do the job. Find Rivendale. That's all.

The thoughts drove him out of bed, and he scraped a razor over his chin and combed his hair. Doing push-ups on the narrow stretch of linoleum flooring, he planned out the next action. The rooftop. Tucker wanted something there; he'd camped out in that old building for a purpose. He had to figure out why. Cops were probably finished with the crime scene by now. It wouldn't hurt to drive over and check it out while they were waiting for Uttley to return from his errand. He'd felt the ripple in his gut again, the unease that Uttley wasn't on the up-and-up and that Mason was covering for him.

When he finished the push-ups followed by a series of crunches, he texted Reggie and arranged to meet him to compare notes. No need to go into detail until they met face-to-face.

Reggie did not reply. Not surprising, as the man required his "beauty sleep" as he put it. Reggie had always been vain about his hair, dying the gray away, and his clothes. It must have been hard for him to adjust to losing an eye. He knew how hard it was for some of the marines he'd worked with to face their disfiguring injuries. Again the anger rose in his gut like bile. Reggie wasn't perfect, but he hadn't deserved to be half blinded. It was time for Tucker to finally be brought to justice.

Finally, the kitchen light flicked on in Keeley's house. Mick tucked in his shirt, ready to go until he saw the knife, nestled in its sheath in the bottom of his bag.

Reggie's admonition echoed in his mind. *You don't have a gun? How are you gonna take him out before he kills the girl?* He didn't want to pick up that knife, to admit to himself that he might actually have to take a life again.

But if Keeley's life hung in the balance?

Or June's?

Quickly he fastened the knife at his waist and threw on a flannel shirt to cover it. When he knocked softly on the door, Keeley opened it immediately and ushered him into the toast-scented kitchen.

She handed him a plate and a cup of coffee. "You're probably going to get tired of toast. I know how to make enchiladas, too, but they aren't good breakfast material."

"Toast is great." He eyed her laptop. "Been busy?"

She grinned. "I sent off the pictures I took last night, thanks to you, so at least I'll get paid for that."

Her grin was infectious, so innocent and joyful. He wanted to imprint it in his memory so he could experience it again and again after she was no longer in his life. Something poked at his heart. "Happy to help."

"The sanctuary really is an amazing place. I can see why your family loves it there."

"You're welcome anytime." What would it be like to have her regular presence on the property? He'd show her the overlook where there was a breathtaking view of the waterfowl during the migratory season. She'd smile and let loose with one of those carefree laughs, and maybe throw her arms around him, and they'd experience the wonder together. He shook the insane thoughts away. *Quit daydreaming, Hudson. Your time with Keeley is ticking down, and that's how it's supposed to be.*

"I'm going to help John today right after I call Junie, so I'll be gone for a little while."

John? It took him a moment. John Bender. He realized he was frowning, so he tried to cover by drinking coffee. He downed most of the cup in one gulp. She refilled it.

"I'll take you over to his clinic. Wait in the truck, if you don't want company."

"I think I'll already have Officer Mason following me. I know you were going to talk to Reggie. Uttley called, and he'll meet us at noon at the station."

Mick drank more coffee. Should he leave her alone with the vet?

Keeley sipped her own coffee, regarding him with raised eyebrows. "I've known John for years."

"He's made some strange decisions, showing up on that rooftop, not calling the cops right away."

"He's not a law enforcement type, Mick. He was LeeAnn's boss, and he loved her."

"I guess that's what bothers me. He loved her, but she loved Tucker. He doesn't seem to get that, or is it me that's mixed up?"

"No." Keeley chewed on her lip. "He made no secret to LeeAnn about how he felt, and it almost made her quit her job at the clinic, but they came to an understanding. She wasn't in love with John and never would be, and he finally accepted that."

Did he? "Would be hard on a man, to be in love with a woman who didn't love him back, and have her so close all the time." It was unnatural, in his opinion, to let the situation continue.

"He settled for friendship for her, and—" Keeley frowned "—hatred for Tucker. He would tell her all the time that Tucker was no good, a louse, until she said if he didn't stop she would quit. After that, he kept his thoughts to himself."

Mick didn't reply, but Keeley must have seen doubt on his face.

"I trust him, and I've worked at the clinic since…" She trailed off.

Since LeeAnn's murder. The coffee burned in his gut.

"If you're sure," he said, jaw tight.

"Yes, I'm sure."

He waited until she was ready to go, and opened the door of her Jeep for her.

"See you later," she said.

He watched Mason follow along behind. Mick drove to the cabin, where he found Reggie sitting amid a messy pile of papers and cruise brochures. He waved a colorful ad at Mick. "Panama or Hawaii? Which one would Nadine like better? She's really actually contacted a lawyer this time, so I've got to step up my game."

"Not that I'm an expert in women…" Mick started.

"Clearly not."

"But again, how is a vacation going to fix your marriage?"

Reggie threw down the brochures. "It will give us quality time to focus on each other so she can remember why she married me in the first place. My charm, my wit, intellect."

"Humility."

He laughed, then his face grew sober. "She's a good woman. I know this job has hardened me, given me a cynical side that's just plain ugly."

Mick nodded. Law enforcement did that.

"It's not fun to be married to me, especially after the Tucker incident. I try to make it up to her with things, a new car and such, but I know at the end of the day she still feels as though she's married to somebody she doesn't like." He sighed. "I told her when I retire, things will be different, if she can just stick it out a little longer."

"Can't picture you retired."

Reggie laughed. "I like to give her hope that things will improve."

"You're still the same guy she married," Mick said. "Down deep somewhere."

"Always the optimist, Mick," Reggie said quietly. "That's why we're here right now."

It was. His disastrous optimistic view of Tucker Rivendale. "But isn't that why we got into the business in the first place? Believing that people can pay for their mistakes and be rehabilitated?"

"Pie in the sky." His tone grew sad. "How many sob stories have we heard? Parolees who promised up and down they were on the right path and wound up in jail again in less than a year? All those pretty promises that turn out to be lies."

And that was where he failed with Tucker, not being able to see through those false promises.

I'm going to make a good life for me and Lee-Ann, Tucker had said. The memory tortured Mick, the smile, the strong handshake. *Thanks for believing in me, man. You're the only guy who ever did.* Mick blinked back to the present to find Reggie staring at him.

"What happens when you've got too many years on the job and you can't sort out lies from truth? Even in yourself?"

The silence stretched between them. "I don't know, Reg. I have no answers."

"Yeah, me, neither." Reggie let loose with a bone-cracking stretch and sank back onto the sofa. "Enough soul-searching. Let's get down to business."

Mick sat and told Reggie all the details about Charlie and Bruce.

"So Ginny is gone, you think? Skipped town, maybe?" Reggie asked.

"Probably, but she has or had some type of connection to the brothers. Maybe Rivendale does, too. They might be in the same business. The brothers were suspected of running a chop shop, and Rivendale is the best at jacking cars."

Reggie's good eye narrowed. "Let me call a buddy of mine. Chop shops are his specialty. I'll run it down."

"Going up to the roof."

"Haven't released the crime scene. I checked."

"I'll check again."

Reggie considered. "Fair enough. Where's Keeley?"

"With John Bender."

"Bender." The pause spoke volumes. "What a guy."

"Don't trust him, either?"

"I don't trust anyone and until we catch Rivendale, and you shouldn't, either." Reggie walked him to the door and gripped his forearm. "He'll kill you if he gets the chance. Don't give him that opportunity."

Mick nodded. "I don't intend to."

FOURTEEN

Keeley breathed in the smell of antiseptic as she stepped into the back room affectionately dubbed Bird ER. John was filling a feeder attached to the side of a seven-foot wire aviary in which the iridescent Anna's hummingbird zipped back and forth, observing his actions with curiosity.

John smiled at her. "It's so much easier now that she doesn't need syringe feeding. I think another week or so and she'll be ready for release." His face grew sad. "I was just thinking how much LeeAnn loved to care for baby hummingbirds. Remember when we had six at one time? She camped out on the floor in a sleeping bag to feed them all."

Keeley's throat thickened at the memory. She'd taken care of June at nighttime so LeeAnn could tend to the babies, no bigger than bumblebees. Thanks to LeeAnn's tenacity, they had all survived, every last precious bird. Keeley made a mental note to tell June about her mama and the baby birds. Maybe she could bring June to the clinic next week if Tucker was caught. It seemed a long shot, but she held on to it. Her life had to return to normal at some point.

John looked so crestfallen, she put her hand on his shoulder. "She would have been happy that this hummer is almost ready to see the world."

He cleared his throat. "Yes, she would have been."

Keeley did not want to indulge any other memories. Her heart was filled with the twin emotions of fear for Junie and tenderness for Mick. Mick... There he was again in her thoughts. If she didn't end the situation soon, her heart might be compromised.

There was no room for anyone but Junie.

None.

She set to work cleaning the cages of the downy woodpecker that was recovering from crashing into a glass door and a kestrel that was still underweight, probably ill from consuming a poisoned rodent. The pair of baby crows that had been saved from a menacing cat would be ready to be released soon. They squawked their disapproval of her presence.

John worked on updating his notes for each bird, in that meticulous, exacting way that made him a superb avian vet. She gazed at the pictures on the wall: photos of the birds rescued at the Bender Veterinary Clinic, and the staff. There was a photo of

John standing next to an older man, both smiling stiffly in front of a neat stucco building.

"Is that your dad?"

He started. "Yes. I worked at his vet clinic for a while."

"Why didn't you two go into partnership? Bender and Bender."

He shrugged. "Sounds like a law firm. Anyway, we don't see eye to eye on things. He thinks he knows the right way to do everything, and he won't ever listen."

"There can't be two head chefs in the kitchen?"

"Especially when one is wrong most of the time." He continued writing, the mechanical pencil held delicately between his fingers.

Keeley swept up some feathers that littered the floor, one a bright green. She thought about a question she'd never asked John.

"What ever happened to the bird LeeAnn was rescuing?"

John started. "What?"

"The day she was killed. You called her and told her about an injured Quaker parrot in the feral colony, didn't you?"

"Yes. I was busy, but she went immediately to see what she could do." He looked at the floor. "I wish that I had gone with her."

"How did you know about the bird? It was early in the morning." She remembered it was a time when Junie was spending the night with her auntie

Keeley. It gave her a pang to remember how she'd once been a mere auntie to the child.

He nodded. "Before six. Someone called the vet clinic and left a message after hours the night before, explaining they'd seen an injured feral parrot."

"Who was it? One of your patients?"

"No. They didn't leave a name."

"So what happened to the parrot?"

He tapped the pencil gently on his file. "I don't know. The cops said there was no sign of her ever having made it to the rooftop." His mouth hardened. "For some insane reason, she met up with Tucker somewhere and they fought. He killed her before she could ever reach the building, most likely. Beast that he is."

"Did you ever go back to check for the wounded bird?"

"Yes, as a matter of fact, when I could bring myself to do it, but I didn't see any sign of an injured parrot."

Keeley swept the feathers into the dust pan. "There's a guy, isn't there, who sort of cares for that colony? What's his name?"

"Meeker, I think. Meeker something. Haven't seen him around in a while." He put the file folder into a tidy drawer. "Why are you thinking about the parrot?"

"I don't know. I guess everything that's happened lately has brought that day back in living color."

"Painful."

"Yes."

"People tell me," he said carefully, "that the best thing to do is move on, don't dwell on the past." His eyes shimmered with pain. "Have you been able to do it?"

"Not fully. You?"

He shook his head. "LeeAnn is perfect."

She didn't correct his verb tense.

"There isn't another woman like her," he said.

Keeley agreed. She wouldn't have even been able to make it this far if God hadn't delivered June into her lap, but she did not have the luxury of living in the past when He'd tasked her, no, *blessed* her, with the responsibility of her little girl's future. "It's hard, but I don't have a choice. I have to move forward for Junie."

He arched an eyebrow. "I always knew that June was LeeAnn's, even though she tried to keep it a secret."

"You did? You didn't let on that you knew until after she died."

"I would never do anything to give Tucker power over LeeAnn or her child. He isn't a father."

She sighed. "Thank you for honoring her decision."

"And he's come back for June now, hasn't he?"

She nodded.

His mouth tightened into a line. "I'll do whatever I can to protect you both."

"Thank you. We're under pretty close watch at the moment."

John rapped the file on the desktop. "Don't trust him."

"Who?"

"The parole officer. Don't rely on him for help, Keeley. He set Tucker loose to kill LeeAnn. He knows it. You can see the guilt in his eyes."

She felt herself wanting to defend Mick, but nothing John said was untrue. "He's not a bad man. He made a mistake, the same mistake LeeAnn made in trusting Tucker."

"LeeAnn was blinded by love. She would have come to her senses eventually. Mick has no such excuse. It was his job to know better."

The hummingbird flitted back and forth, looking for freedom, perhaps. She wondered how Mick would feel if he was freed from the ponderous burden of guilt that weighed him down. Try as she might to keep him out of her thoughts, his face kept appearing in her mind's eye.

You've got to stop that, she thought. She would not spend time worrying about Mick Hudson.

John's hard stare bored into her.

"You like him, don't you?"

She tightened her grip on the broom handle.

"I guess I wish Tucker's actions hadn't ruined him, too, but there's nothing I can do about that. I have to take care of myself and Junie."

"Yes, that's all that matters. Family. Remember that I'm always here for you." He flushed a deep scarlet and looked away. "Sorry. I miss her so much, sometimes I can almost feel her presence." Tears glittered beneath his lowered lashes.

How much they'd all suffered. At least she had Junie. John had nothing but his birds. "Thank you, John," she said. "You are a good friend."

He nodded, gathering his folders without meeting her eyes.

She continued on with her rounds, freshening bedding material and filling feeding cups. The green feather stayed on her mind. Had the parrot somehow survived its injury? Or had it lost its life the same day as her beautiful sister?

Why had she never thought of it before?

Mick met Keeley at the house. He didn't ask how her time had gone with John Bender, though he burned to do so. She fixed peanut-butter-and-banana sandwiches for an early lunch before their meeting with Chief Uttley.

"I'm out of jelly," she explained. He noticed she was also out of milk and eggs.

"This is good," he said. He'd never eaten that particular combination and he was surprised that he liked it. He wasn't sure if it was the food or the woman who'd fixed it for him that made him enjoy it. When his phone buzzed, he answered.

"It's Pickford. Dug something up you might be able to use."

Mick was surprised. He had not thought the sheriff would actually follow through with checking out Uttley.

"My buddies had nothing much to say about Uttley. About ten years ago, though, he killed a female pedestrian while he was in pursuit of a suspect. Took a lot out of him. One of those bad things and not his fault. Other than that, they got nothing bad to say, and if they did they aren't going to blab it."

He understood. The blue brotherhood. There might be a whole lot of things Pickford's buddies weren't ready to share. "Thank you."

"And there's one more thing that might interest you. One of my guys knew of the brother Bruce."

"From the garage?"

"Yeah. Said his cop cousin busted Brother Bruce a year ago for misdemeanor stuff here in Oregon, but he always knew the kid was into something they couldn't prove."

No news there. He was about to end the call.

"I guess you can ask your former colleagues about it. Looks like your outfit handled his parole."

Mike squeezed the phone to his ear. "What?"

Pickford paused. "I think you heard me. Maybe you should spend more time looking at your own people than rustling up dirt in our departments."

"Who was his parole officer?"

"Guy named Reginald Donaldson. Know him?"

It seemed as if all the air was sucked out of the room. "Yes, I know him," Mick said. "Thanks again."

He disconnected and stared at the phone in his hands. Reggie was Brother Bruce's parole officer? Why had he concealed the fact? He sent a text.

Need to talk to you this afternoon.

There was no response.

Keeley frowned. "You look as if you just lost your best friend."

Had he? No sense piling on to her worries until he'd checked it out. "Something I need to do later."

"Okay."

She went into her bedroom to grab a sweater and came immediately back with frown. "You fixed the window."

He nodded.

"I told you it would have to wait."

"Forecasting rain. You needed a window. I know a guy. It was cheap."

She yanked on the sweater. "I didn't want that. I told you I wasn't going to replace it. Did you even hear what I said?" Storm clouds drifted through her eyes.

He shrugged. "You needed it."

"I need a lot of things," she snapped. "I need a

new car and the roof fixed and a killer to be caught and my life to get back to normal, but I can't rely on someone else to suddenly fix everything for us." Her voice rose with each word.

"I wanted to help."

"So did he."

"Who?"

"Tucker." Her voice vibrated with emotion. "He fixed my car, hung pictures for my sister. She, we, let him into our lives." Tears glittered, illuminating that blue of her irises to sapphire. "We let him in, don't you see? We trusted him."

Mick's heart felt as though it had been sliced with a cleaver. Why hadn't he thought it out before he'd barreled ahead and went against her wishes? Big clumsy brute shoving his way in, knowing what was best for a woman who'd been betrayed by another brute not two years before. He let out a long slow breath. "I didn't think."

Her arms were folded, shoulders high and tight, cheeks flooded with color. "You can't come in here and interfere. I need you to help me catch Tucker, nothing more. Do you understand?"

He realized that he'd also managed to shame her, expose her vulnerability in ways that made her feel small and inadequate. Worst of all, he'd scared her. *You're an idiot, Mick.* He stood and said the only thing he could. "I apologize. Sincerely."

Her lips thinned into a tight line, nostrils flared as she fought for breath. "Never mind. Let's go meet the chief. I want this thing resolved as soon as possible."

"So I can get you out of my life," he knew she meant. He didn't blame her.

Mick Hudson, Class A jerk, was muddying the waters far more than he was helping. He thought about how she'd feel if she knew the anonymous money came from him every month. He knew how she'd see it. Interference, another way a man was prying into her life without invitation. He'd have to tell her, but maybe not until she'd paid off a few bills with the next check. At least he could give her that.

She walked by him stiffly, and he followed her to the truck, his spirit fallen to dirt level, worry about Reggie warring with regret at hurting Keeley.

In the truck, it was deadly silent.

"Again," he said, clearing his throat, "I am sorry. I didn't think about how you'd feel. I was wrong."

She looked out the window. "I know you meant well. It was easy to misunderstand when I said Junie and I needed you."

"I overstepped. No excuse."

Why had he thought to do it anyway? Because he couldn't stand the idea that she might be unsafe, compromised by the storm and whatever other forces were out to hurt her. It was one thing, one small thing that he could do to make her life better, and for some reason she was all he could think about.

Or maybe it was just because he was an over-bearing jerk, one of those chauvinists who felt as if a woman needed a man to take care of them. "No," he wanted to say. "I know you are strong, so strong it takes my breath away." He couldn't say it. The only thing to do was get the meeting over with and get to the bottom of things with Reggie.

He cranked the engine to life. She pressed her hands to her mouth and gave a little half sigh and then, suddenly, she'd scooted over and put her arms around his neck.

He was so startled he didn't know what to do. His mind could not understand, but his body re-acted, embracing her, relishing the softness of hers, the brush of her orange-shampoo-scented hair, the tickle of her lashes against his jaw. He was too sur-prised to speak, to rouse her from whatever impulse had caused her sudden change of heart.

"I'm sorry," she whispered. "You were being generous, and I made you feel bad," she mumbled into his T-shirt.

He wrapped his arms around her tighter, letting the feel of her press some life back into his battered heart. "My fault. Totally. You had every right to be mad. I was a jerk."

She put her head against his chest and he thought the thundering of his heart might deafen her. He heard her sigh, long and slow, a sound that was more tender and soft than the peeping of baby birds. He breathed in the warmth of her. If there was one moment in his life that he could hold on to forever, this was the one.

"Thank you for replacing my window." She took a breath before she pulled away, and he felt bereft. "That's all I should have said. An act of kindness is not going to strip away my independence or threaten Junie's safety. I've been scared since Lee-Ann's death. Too scared. My mother used to say if you decline a gift, you rob the giver of a blessing. Anyway," she said, buckling her seat belt, "Thank you."

He was nonplussed, thrown completely off-kilter by her sincerity, the ease at which she expressed herself and bared her heart. He would have said anything then to make her lay her head down against him again, to be so close to something so incredibly wonderful. What was happening to him?

It was a relief to start the engine and watch the miles tick away, but even so his pulse refused to return to a normal rhythm. When his phone rang, he snatched it up as if it was a parachute rip cord and he was plummeting. "Hello?"

There was the sound of breathing, heavy and panicked.

"You have to help her."

His nerves iced over. "Tucker?"

Keeley pressed close to hear.

"At the garage. I don't think she's going to make it," Tucker gasped.

"Who? What happened? Tell me," he commanded.

"Just hurry." There was a soft, high-pitched moan and the phone disconnected.

Mick stared at the phone in his hand.

Keeley's face was white. "It has to be the Quick Stop Garage. Is he talking about Ginny? That sounded like a woman in pain."

"Call the police."

She was already reaching for the phone.

His mind whirled. "We're only six blocks away. I'll drop you at the next light."

"No. He's talking about Ginny and she's hurt. I'm coming."

"This could all be a trap, Keeley. Consider the source."

"That was fear in Tucker's voice, Mick. Terror even. He wasn't faking that. We have to go now."

He drove as fast as he could, slowing just before the entrance to the garage. There was no glimmer of light from the darkened window. He jerked the truck to a stop. This time, he wasn't worried about politeness.

"Listen to me, you're a mother now, the only person Junie has in this world." He gripped her upper arms and would not let her look away. "You can't go in there. Keep the engine running and stay locked in until the cops arrive."

"I…" Her eyes searched his. He saw the struggle there, and the decision born of love for her little girl. "Okay."

As he got out she clutched at his hand. "You

shouldn't go in, either, Mick. You're not a parole officer anymore."

"I still have one case left to close," he said. *For you and Junie*. Before he could reconsider, he pressed a kiss to her forehead before he ran toward the back entrance of the garage.

Mick could see nothing in the two windows he checked. He estimated it would be less than ten minutes before the police would arrive. The reasonable thing to do would be to wait, but he was in no mood to be reasonable, not after he'd heard that moan of pain.

Tucker Rivendale would not hurt anyone else if Mick could help it.

The only option seemed to be to edge around to the back door and force his way in. He didn't need to. The door was ajar; the small pane of glass above the knob was shattered. He made himself as small a target as he could manage and then crept through. His shoes crunched on the glass. Tucker would know he had arrived, served up like a Christmas goose, but there was no help for it now. He unsheathed the knife. Holding it in front of him, he scooted behind a tool chest, which was barely big enough to cover him. Go for broke. It was the only way to save Ginny, if she was actually in danger.

"Tucker," he yelled into the darkness.

"Here" came the reply from the mechanic's bay. He could see through the threshold into the cavernous space. "Hurry."

Tucker's voice was urgent, plaintive. So sincere. *Don't fall for it again, Mick*. He eased closer, keeping sheltered as much as he could. He saw what he was looking for, the switch to the overhead lights. It would give him one moment of surprise only, but a moment might be all he would need to ascertain if the whole thing was a ploy to get to Keeley.

He slammed the switch up and the lights buzzed on.

Inside, next to a car with no wheels, was Tucker Rivendale.

On the floor next to him was Ginny's crumpled body.

FIFTEEN

The police would be there in moments. Keeley could hear the siren in the distance, but there were so many avenues of escape for Tucker. What if he fled into the woods? Escaped from Mick after— she swallowed hard—he killed him. Mick was only walking into that garage to protect her and June, and now Ginny. He would die if it meant that they might have a chance to live a life free of Tucker. Her stomach tightened to fist size.

She threw the door open and ran, vowing that she would keep to the shelter of the trees behind the garage and wait for the police. If Tucker fled that way, she could at least inform them which way he'd gone. Or maybe she'd spot something, anything that might create a distraction so Mick could get Ginny out safely. The hammering of her pulse increased with each passing moment.

She raced to the back and spotted the open door. Her heart ached to scream his name. *Mick, what's happening in there?* She crept close enough to peer inside.

She saw Tucker step into her line of sight, hands held up in the air. Her breath caught. Mick had done it; somehow he'd thrown Tucker off guard. She sprinted inside, a cry escaping when she saw Ginny lying on the stained cement floor.

Mick shot her a look. He had a knife in his hand.

She knelt next to Ginny, whose face was bruised and her lip split. A faint pulse beat in her wrist but her body was cold, so cold.

Tucker's mouth was twisted in grief. "You've got to save her. She's just a kid. She was trying to help me."

"Why did you do this to her?" Mick snarled, voice barely recognizable as the big-hearted man she knew.

"I didn't hurt her," Tucker said. "She texted to tell me the brothers, the guys who own this garage, brought her here. I broke in and found her like this. I didn't know who else to call. I figured the cops would shoot me on sight."

Mick's knife-armed hand didn't waver. "They might anyway."

Tucker shook his head. "If that's the way it ends, so be it, but just help Ginny, okay? Can you stop trying to ruin me long enough to do that? She's my friend."

Keeley took off her jacket and put it over the girl, trying to chafe some warmth back into her hands.

"Help is coming, Ginny," she crooned in the same tone she used when Junie was scared about thunder. "Hang in there."

The sirens screamed now, just outside the building.

Tucker shifted from foot to foot. Would he try to run? She wasn't sure, but she knew Mick would not let him leave the garage under any circumstances.

Tucker finally tore his gaze away from Ginny and stared at her.

"Ginny told me June was my kid. I just wanted to get to know her better. I came here so I could tell her that I'm not the man everybody thinks I am. That's all. I never meant to scare you. I'm not a killer."

Keeley met his gaze, saw the sorrow there. Was he deluded enough to think himself innocent? Was it possible that he could not face what he had done? The thought that had lived in the darkest part of her soul for so many months found its way past her lips.

"LeeAnn loved you."

He swallowed hard. "I loved her, too, more than anything."

Keeley sucked in a breath. "Tucker, why did you kill my sister? Why?"

The noise of the sirens echoed and bounced through the cavernous garage, but her attention remained riveted on Tucker.

"Why did you kill my sister?" she repeated.

He closed his eyes, mouth twisted as if he was in physical pain. When he opened them, his face blazed with emotion. Each syllable fell like a stone. "I did not kill LeeAnn."

The air seemed to leave the room, pulling the oxygen from her lungs. Tucker Rivendale, her enemy, her sister's killer, sounded very much like a man telling the truth.

Mick edged closer. "No more. You'll have your say in court."

Tucker laughed, an edge of hysteria in it. "I won't live to see a courtroom, Mick. You'll see to that, won't you?"

"What are you talking about?" Mick snapped. His profile was hard as granite, his whole body tense.

"Freeze! Police!" Chief Uttley charged in, gun aimed at Tucker.

Tucker leaped backward, whether scared or intending to flee, Keeley didn't know.

Uttley fired two shots. The explosion was deafening. Mick covered Keeley and Ginny with his body, gripping them in a desperate embrace. She heard running feet as more officers entered.

Sounds echoed around her. Shouting, intense, energy charged. Radios buzzed and crackled. Mick's breathing, as uncertain as her own.

"Don't move," he murmured.

He pressed close, and she was grateful for his strong chest, heart beating fast and steady.

When her ears stopped ringing, he eased off her. She stayed on her knees, clutching Ginny's hand.

Mick stood between her and Uttley. The lines around his mouth were pronounced, relief and despair mixing in his expression.

Uttley knelt and stared at Ginny, gun still in his hand.

"Is she alive?"

Keeley nodded. "But hurt badly. I can hardly feel her pulse."

"Paramedics are two minutes out." He reached out a finger and gently brushed the dark hair from Ginny's face. "You're gonna be fine, Virginia. Just fine," he said.

So Uttley had been covering for Ginny. They'd been right.

"How do you know her?" Keeley asked quietly.

His eyes burned as he stared at the fallen girl. "Ten years ago, I killed her mother."

Horror trickled through Keeley.

He asked, without taking his eyes off Ginny, "May I hold her hand?"

Keeley moved aside so Uttley could get closer. Mick helped her to her feet, standing very close.

She looked at Mick and the bustling cops that filled the space.

"How…?" She swallowed. "What happened to Tucker?"

Mick moved her toward the door. "Let's go outside."

She resisted. "I want to know."

"It's better to wait outside."

She let him lead her, but at the last moment, she turned to look. There over the shoulder of another medic and Officer Mason, Tucker lay on the ground, head turned toward them, one arm outstretched as if he yearned for someone to take it. Blood seeped through the front of his shirt.

He'd been shot. An unarmed man. Her sister's killer. Keeley's head spun and the ground rose up to meet her.

Mick carried Keeley outside and helped her sit on a fallen log. She put her face into his shirtfront and sobbed.

He let her cry, cradling her close, his own mind trying to process the finality of what had just occurred. It was done. Finally. Tucker Rivendale had been brought to justice. But Tucker had been unarmed, shot in cold blood.

Nonetheless, the man was a murderer. He should have felt elated, relieved, but instead he had the sensation that everything inside him had turned to stone. It was the same feeling he'd gotten looking down at the grave of the son he'd never even known about, a regret so heavy it sank his soul to the depths.

He realized that however things had turned out, no matter how much past history was piled up, he'd believed Tucker. The worst thing was, way down deep, in the very tiniest sliver of his drowned soul, he still did. Had Tucker really thought Mick would murder him rather than see him safely to prison?

I did not kill LeeAnn.

Said the man with yet another woman lying broken at his feet. Tucker would have babbled anything that might have bought him time or a chance at escape. Mick could not fathom why he still had doubts. He focused on Keeley, willing some of her pain into his body. He rubbed his hands over her back and shoulders, feeling the sobs that rattled through her. One woman, too much grief that she didn't deserve.

Let me take it for her, God. Let this be on me.

It had been a very long time since he'd spoken to God. He was not sure God was even listening, not anymore. Mick was locked away in a jail of his own making, and he figured God had better things to do than chase after one washed-up paroled officer. He stroked her hair, rubbed her shoulders and pressed his cheek to the top of her head.

"I'm sorry," he said, without knowing why. "I'm so sorry."

Keeley sucked in a shuddering breath and pulling away to look at him. "Did you hear what Tucker said?"

"Yes."

"What if he was telling the truth?" she whispered.

He swallowed. "He wasn't."

"Are you sure?"

She searched his face, tears glittering like a sunlit pond.

He could not say what she wanted to hear. He could only lose himself in the shimmering blue of her grief. He pressed a kiss on her cheek, soft and satin, and wiped the tears away. "Keeley, it's over. Hang on to that. You're safe, June is safe. It's all over."

He felt himself leaning toward her, wanting nothing more than to cover her mouth with an unending kiss. Heart pounding, he saw her face tip to his. Her lips just touched his, and the yearning inside him nearly overwhelmed his sense.

Officer Mason approached, his face grim. Mick broke away. What had he been about to do?

"Do you need medical care?" Mason said. "Either one of you?"

Mick checked with Keeley, who shook her head. "No. We're okay."

Mason didn't respond, scrutinizing the tree line as if he was tracking a felon.

"Uttley said he'd killed Ginny's mother," Mick said quietly.

Mason chewed his lip, still gazing at the treetops. "When he was a new cop. He was in pursuit of a suspect and she was in the crosswalk. Tragic accident. She lived for a few days. Uttley promised to look out for her daughter, Virginia. She was ten at the time. Went to live with her aunt, but Uttley kept tabs on her, helped her out when he could over the years."

Keeley sighed, a long sad sound.

"Ginny's been in and out of trouble. Did some jail time for drugs. Showed up here a few months ago. Uttley was worried she was into something. Started hanging out at the garage. We've never gotten them on anything, but those brothers are into something bad, and Uttley was worried about Ginny. She asked him about Rivendale's case, but she refused to say why."

"That's why he covered for her at the newspaper building. He was afraid she was consorting with Tucker, too."

Mason shrugged. "That's all I'm going to say. He's a good man and a good cop and you'll have to get the rest from him. There's going to be an investigation now and things are going to come out. I've got to go." He left to speak to the other officers emerging from the garage.

The medics rolled out a stretcher. Keeley looked away and swallowed hard. Mick gripped her shoulder. A second ambulance pulled up, and Ginny was loaded on board.

What followed was an excruciating round of questioning before they headed to the police station for yet another session. Mick's mind whirled in many different directions.

Keeley was dead silent as they drove to the

station. Finally, when they pulled into the lot, she spoke.

"Mick, after this, after we're done with the police, would you take me to see June? Please? I need to be with her."

"Yes." He realized in that moment he would do absolutely anything she asked. Period. It scared him.

She nodded, relief relaxing her features. "I've missed her so much."

"I know." Again he felt the pang, that odd pinch that came when he considered the parent-child bond. He'd never had a chance to love his son, hadn't even known he had produced one, so he wondered sometimes what that strange feeling could be. Regret? Envy? Or was it possible that God had wired him to love a child, even though he'd never gotten to meet him? He shook himself, unsure why his thoughts turned ever more frequently to God.

Now it was not Chief Uttley in charge of the investigation, but a new man in his sixties who introduced himself as Chief Allen as he called Mick into Uttley's office. Mick gave Keeley's hand a squeeze as he left.

"I'm just stepping in to help out," Allen said, his head shaved bald and speckled with sunspots. His posture was perfect, uniform neat.

Mick knew. Uttley had been removed, pending

an investigation into both the shooting and his covering up for Ginny.

Allen listened patiently, taking notes on a yellow notepad as Mick talked. When Mick was done, Allen smiled. "I've been doing this for a long time, Mr. Hudson, practically a lifetime, but before I took on this job I was a major in the corps."

Mick found himself sitting straighter. "I thought so, sir."

Allen laughed. "Now that we've established a rapport, I already had a talk with Sheriff Pickford, who seems to think you don't completely trust the cops."

"Uttley was covering up something that might have helped us catch Tucker earlier, sir."

"And he'll be disciplined for that, but he was doing it out of a higher sense of duty. What's the first leadership trait, son?"

"Justice," Mick said automatically.

"Yes, and you and I both know justice is a moving target sometimes."

"Yes, sir."

"So you and your friend—" he consulted his notepad "—Reginald Donaldson, rode into town to capture Tucker Rivendale, like a couple of modern-day cowboys."

"Or marines, sir," Mick said.

Allen laughed again. "Right. So I'm thinking you've been working your own investigation, which is what led you to your father's property where you encountered Virginia and the brothers, Bruce and Charlie."

"Yes, sir."

"Did you know that Reginald was Bruce's former parole officer?"

"I did not, sir, until Sheriff Pickford told me."

"Reginald is on his way here, so we can ask him about that point."

Mick sure wanted to hear Reggie's answer.

"It may have nothing whatever to do with the current situation, of course." Allen tapped a pencil on the desktop. "Then again, when we've got a murder investigation in progress, every point has to be considered."

"Murder, sir?"

"That surprises you?"

"Uttley was apprehending a fugitive. It wasn't murder."

"Second leadership trait of a marine, son?"

"Judgment," Mick fired off.

Allen searched his face. "You trusted this Rivendale, didn't you?"

Mick swallowed hard. "Yes, sir."

"And now you don't think you can trust yourself, your judgment."

Mick stayed quiet.

"You said Rivendale called you, asked for help for Ginny, denied killing LeeAnn Stevens."

"Yes, sir."

"And you think he was trying to lure you there to lay his hands on Keeley Stevens? You believe that?"

Did he? Deep down?

"Your hesitation speaks volumes," Allen said softly. "Still struggling with the judgment issue, I see."

"Sir, with all due respect, but isn't the case closed? Rivendale—" He cleared his throat. "Uttley killed Rivendale to protect Ginny. Isn't that the end of it? Justified shooting."

Allen looked at him closely. "That would be very neat and tidy, except for two things."

Mick stood, feeling somehow that he could face whatever was coming better standing at attention. "What's that, sir?"

"Bruce and Charlie have apparently skipped town, leaving a bag of bloodstained clothes in their back room."

Mick had to fight to keep from gaping. Bloodstained clothes?

Allen folded his hands, staring at Mick. "And Tucker Rivendale is still alive."

The words rang in Mick's head. Still alive. Two stretchers. Tucker was alive. Through a fog he saw Allen still staring at him.

"Virginia is our murder victim. She died on scene."

SIXTEEN

Before she knocked on the door to Aunt Viv's house, Keeley ran her fingers through her hair and blew her nose. Mick hung back behind her, hands in his pockets. She could not string one rational thought together after what had happened, but something inside her did not want to be separated from Mick. Her whole being yearned to be near him, and the thought set her nerves quivering.

Junie. She's the only important thing right now.

After a last deep breath, she rapped on the door.

Viv opened it, face reddened by recent crying. She hugged Keeley. "I'm so grateful that you're safe."

Keeley enjoyed the comfort of Viv's tight hug. "It's terrible. All of it."

Viv let her go. "Derek called and told me the whole story. He's devastated about what happened to Ginny. He tried so hard all these years to care for her. I didn't know a thing about it. I wish I could have helped in some way."

Keeley heard Mick shift on the step behind her.

"Mick…" What could she say about Mick and her strange onslaught of feelings for him? "He drove me over," she finished lamely.

Viv ushered them inside. "Junie's in the backyard."

In a moment, Keeley was out the back sliding door and into the yard, where she found Junie carefully filling her plastic bucket with fallen leaves. She looked up, her face splitting into a wide smile.

Keeley ran to her and gathered her into an embrace. "Junie" was all she could say through the tears. When June wriggled free, she put a chubby hand to Keeley's face.

"Sad?"

Keeley struggled for breath. "No," she lied. "Happy to see you. Happy tears."

June fastidiously wiped Keeley's face with her palms. "Better."

"Yes. Better."

Junie's gaze traveled to Mick. She walked to him, craning her head back to see his face.

Mick immediately took a knee. The sweetness of that gesture broke Keeley's heart all over again. This man, stricken as he was, robbed of the opportunity to be a parent, sank down to the ground at the feet of her little girl.

"Junie, this is Mr. Hudson."

Junie regarded him soberly.

"You can call me Mick. Very nice to meet you,

June." He took her whole hand in three fingers and solemnly shook. Mick pointed to her bucket. "You are collecting leaves."

She nodded.

"You haven't finished yet."

She nodded again. Then she lifted the bucket and he took it, the handle swallowed up by his fingers. Without another word, they set to work, Mick and Junie, collecting all the leaves they could find.

Keeley watched them, flooded with too many emotions to name. She thought about Ginny, who had lost her mother and her way. Uttley, who was now saddled with an even more ponderous weight of guilt. When Junie grinned at a particularly fine leaf specimen that Mick handed over, Keeley's heart lurched when she saw a shadow of Tucker in the expression.

I did not kill LeeAnn.

Why did she want to believe him? He'd murdered her sister. He was a liar. But the police were now pursuing Charlie and Bruce. What if Tucker was telling the truth and he hadn't hurt Ginny? He was now under police protection as the doctors struggled to save his life. And then what? He would go to prison. End of story. Out of their lives forever.

Mick, too? There would be no reason for him to stick around. Her heart squeezed.

Viv went to answer the doorbell and ushered John into the backyard. He embraced Keeley.

"I can't believe they got him. Finally." He heaved out a breath. "Are you okay?"

She returned the hug. "Yes."

"Hey, June bug," he called.

Junie raced over to John and hugged him around the knees before she handed him a leaf.

"Thank you. I will put it in my pocket for safe-keeping. Will you come see the birds at my office soon? They're lonely without you."

Junie nodded before she returned to Mick who shot a wary glance at John before they returned to their leaf hunting.

"So your life will return to normal," he said. "No need for a bodyguard anymore."

"I guess not."

"You'll bring Junie home?"

"For a few days, and then I've got to get back to work. By the end of the summer, I'm hoping to move her in with me permanently."

"That's great." He smiled. "I was just thinking that your sister would be proud of you."

Her eyes filled. "I hope so."

"I know so." His gaze drifted to Junie again. "And Tucker Rivendale will rot in prison. If he survives, that is."

"Before Uttley shot him, he said he didn't do it."

"And you actually buy that?" John huffed. "I will never understand what he has that makes women believe his lies. He's a loser, and even after he killed your sister, you still believe him."

"I didn't say I believed him."

John slapped a hand on his thigh. "You don't need to say it. It's there in your face."

Mick put down his bucket and drew closer.

Keeley lifted her chin. "I lost more than anyone, John."

"You're letting yourself be manipulated, Lee-Ann." His face flushed at the mistake. "I mean Keeley. Wise up, why don't you?"

"Don't speak to her in that tone." Mick's voice was low.

John looked from Mick to Keeley. He started to reply then stopped, heaving out a long breath. "You're right. I'm sorry."

Keeley didn't answer.

John stared at Mick. "But what about you? Do you honestly believe Tucker is innocent?"

"I don't know."

"I guess that would make sense, since it would get you off the hook."

Mick stiffened.

John's face grew thoughtful. "Yeah, if you can convince yourself and Keeley that Tucker's been framed, then you don't have to shoulder the guilt for letting him off house arrest to murder Lee-Ann."

Mick blinked and came closer. "This is not the

place for this conversation," he said. "There's a child within earshot."

John glared. "You don't have to tell me about Junie. I'm here for her like I always have been. Go home, Mr. Hudson. If you want to assuage your guilt with your wild theories, go ahead, but leave Keeley and Junie out of it."

Mick jutted out his chin. "I'm staying until I'm sure everything is wrapped up."

"How long?" John fired back.

"None of your business," Mick snapped.

"Mick," Junie called.

Mick and John remained locked in a stare down for another long moment before Mick broke away to return to June.

John looked at his watch. "I've got to go. Are you driving home now?"

She nodded.

"I'll see you later, then. How about I bring some dinner?"

"That's not necessary."

"I know. I just want to do something to mark the occasion. You're finally getting your life back. You can put the past behind you." He gave her a final hug and left.

Would the past finally be behind her? She'd prayed so long and hard that she would be able to start a new life for Junie, just the two of them, free from the shadow of her sister's murder.

But what if Tucker was telling the truth?

She watched Mick picking up the leaves that dropped from Junie's palms as she tried to squish them into the bucket.

And how would she feel when Mick stepped out of her life forever?

Mick did not want to think about John's accusation, but it stuck in his mind nonetheless. Maybe he was considering the possibility of Tucker's innocence because it relieved him of the burden of guilt.

But there were odd pieces to the puzzle that didn't fit. The rooftop diagram. The bloody clothes left by Bruce and Charlie. And Reggie's involvement with Bruce as his parole officer. He hadn't imagined those facts. Plus he didn't see how Tucker could have sent the fake text from Fred at *Bird's Away Magazine*. It certainly wasn't from the cell phone the police had confiscated at the garage. Mason had let that much slip.

Maybe he was grasping at straws, doing anything he could to stay involved in Keeley's life. It was a sobering thought. Was it his guilt that kept his heart wandering back to her? Or something else?

He listened to Keeley's and June's lively chatter, fascinated. It was so easy and smooth, their conversation, like two birds effortlessly skimming the water. The little girl was buckled in the cramped backseat of his truck; he could just see her flyaway blond hair in the rearview mirror. She swung her toy, Mr. Moo Moo, back and forth. He was pleased to see the cow's missing eye had been reattached. For a moment, he allowed himself to imagine what it would be like to be a father to a family with a child like Junie and a woman like Keeley. Would it be an overwhelming responsibility? A frightening lifelong commitment?

No, he decided. It would be the greatest honor of a man's life.

An honor denied to him.

Someday John might assume that role in Keeley's life. John certainly saw himself as their protector. The thought knifed in Mick's gut. Why not? His conscience taunted him. The guy was a professional. He'd known the type for years. Owned a nice house and a steady practice. Mick found he was clutching the steering wheel in a death grip. He eased off.

Keeley still looked tired, pale, but there was a peacefulness about her that he knew came from having Junie close by.

Junie began to hum.

"Sing?" she said.

Keeley chimed in with something about buses and wheels going around. The melody filled the truck.

Mick could feel June staring at him.

"She wants you to sing, too," Keeley said.

Him? Sing? He never sang or even hummed and with good reason. Birds were known to plummet from the sky within earshot of his horrible crooning. He looked at Junie in the rearview. That little girl wanted a song. *Step up*, he told himself. Then all of a sudden he was rasping along about windshield wipers that swished and doors opening and closing. He sang with as much vigor and commitment as he had shown when his company fought in Khafji in Operation Desert Storm. All in. For her.

When the song was finished, Junie contented herself looking out the window. Mick heaved a sigh of relief. He'd had no idea there were so many things moving and shaking on a bus.

Keeley grinned. "That was the best chorus we've ever sung."

It thrilled him for no particular reason. "No thanks to me."

"It was perfect." Something in the tone was soft and warm and spread through his veins like summer sunshine. She touched his hand.

"Thank you for everything you've done for us."

"Haven't done much."

"Yes, you have, and I won't ever forget it." She paused. "I want you to know that if Tucker did…" She shot a look at Junie. "If he did it, it wasn't your fault. He's convincing. He made LeeAnn believe him, and I think part of me does, too."

"Thank you for saying that."

"I know LeeAnn wouldn't blame you, and I don't, either."

He stared at the road.

"But you still blame yourself." She stroked his

arm, tingles shooting up and down his side. "Mick, even if what happened was out of negligence, or carelessness, or ignorance, God forgives if you ask Him to."

"I've never asked," he found himself saying.

"Because you don't think you're worthy of forgiveness?"

Yes, his heart said, even though he couldn't form the words. *I am not worthy of forgiveness. I am not worthy of you.*

"Mick, you are worthy of God's love. You're bossy and taciturn and kind of a maddening driver, but God forgives everything because you're His son."

He blinked.

"If your own son had lived, do you think you would have forgiven the mistakes he made in his life?"

His own son. His boy. "I don't know. I never got the chance to find out."

"Well, I know, because when God gave us Junie I learned that I would forgive her a million times over because I love her. People are meant to love and forgive because God made us that way. I think it's the one really good thing about us."

"But you are good, Keeley. You are kind and gentle and committed and honest with your emotions." He could not believe that the feelings in his heart had found words to accompany them. "You're…good."

"And I've got just as many sins as you, Mick," she said quietly. "They're just different."

"And you believe God forgives them?"

The conversation with his father came back to him.

"Your mom would have said guilt is a prison and God put the key in your hand. All you need to do is take it and let yourself loose."

What would it be like to let himself out of the cage of guilt? Would he be free to let joy into his life? To open his heart like Keeley did? To a child? To love? The thought tantalized him. They pulled up to Keeley's driveway.

"I'm going to think about it, what you said."

She smiled. "I'm glad." As they got out, Keeley helped June open the mailbox.

Keeley gave a huge sigh when she saw the legal-size envelope.

"I don't know who sends this money, but it always saves me in the nick of time." She squinted at the envelope. Slowly her gaze slid to him. She knew.

"Mick, is this from you?"

He saw the slow anger kindling in her eyes, and he wanted to deny it. "Yes, ma'am," he said softly.

"Why?"

"I knew you needed it. Your debts…"

Her face blanched. "You researched my debts?"

"I wanted to help you, to make up for…" His

words betrayed him, like they always did. He watched her face ice over.

"You thought you could make it up to me? My sister's murder?"

"No," he said, hating his own tongue. "I didn't mean that. I wanted to take care of you."

"All this time. You never said a word. How long were you going to keep up the lie?"

He clenched his hands into fists. "I thought..."

"Oh, right. You thought you were taking care of me. It's the same thing John tries to do all the time, take care of us. So did Tucker. Well, you know what? We don't need to be taken care of. Junie and I are fine, and we don't need your charity."

"I know that."

"And we don't need you hanging around here out of guilt."

It's not guilt, he wanted to say. *Not anymore.*

She held up the check. "Here."

"I meant it to help you."

"Take it back to your sanctuary and use it for the birds."

"Keeley..."

She shoved the check into his hands and tugged Junie to the house.

He crushed the paper in his fists, wondering how he'd once again managed to mess up the best thing in his life. Keeley, he realized through the tide of grief, was the only woman he'd trusted enough to open up to. It had started out of guilt, a sense of duty, but now as he watched her close the door, he realized that she meant something else to him.

Too little. Too late. He should have that tattooed on his chest. There was nothing else to be done except for him to get into his truck and leave, but not before he talked to Reggie and looked into the nagging details that still bothered him about the Tucker situation. He'd turned to go back to the truck when the door of the house was flung open. Keeley had June in her arms, and she deposited her gently on the front step.

"Stay here for a minute." She hesitated, looking helplessly around before reluctantly eyeing Mick. "Can you make sure she doesn't wander off? Just watch her, that's all. I wouldn't ask, but…"

He nodded and joined Junie on the porch. "What's wrong?"

She shook her head and returned to the house. The hair on the back of his neck prickled, but he dutifully took up his position next to June.

June sat down on the weathered porch and started trying to take off her socks and shoes, which Mick noticed were soaking wet. She grunted, and her cheeks flushed red with the effort.

He knelt down and helped her until the shoes and wet socks were off. She sighed and hopped down the first porch step.

"Mama said to stay on the porch," he said.

A crafty look came over her face, and she hopped down the next step.

"June, you gotta do what your Mama says."

June hopped down the last step and started to sprint away when Mick caught her up as gently as he could. She squirmed at first until he positioned her on his shoulders. "Okay, Miss June. Mind your head," he said as he ducked through the front door, June giggling madly and bouncing on his shoulders.

He noticed the water immediately, soaked floorboards outside the kitchen. Keeley emerged from the hallway, her pants rolled up and shoes discarded. She eyed Junie. "I told you to…"

"She decided to disregard your orders," he cut in. "What's going on?"

"Someone turned on all the taps in the kitchen and the bathroom and stoppered up the sinks and tub. Everything is soaked." There was a slight tremble in her voice, but she did not cry. "Who would do that?"

Who indeed? "Couldn't have been Tucker." A sinister thought rose in his mind. John Bender was determined to pull Keeley into his orbit, and Junie, too. "Would Bender do something like this?"

She started as if she'd gotten an electric shock. "John? Of course not. He cares for us. How could you think such a thing?"

The Molotov cocktail. A house left to flood. Both designed to push her out of her house and into his. "He wants you to move in with him."

She exploded. "Mick, stop it," she shouted. "I

told you no one is going to pressure me into doing anything. This is my house, for me and Junie. There's no room for anyone else in our lives."

Junie shoved her fingers in her mouth and pressed her face against the top of Mick's head, eyes closed, whimpering.

Keeley's face crumpled. "Oh, honey. I'm sorry."

"Mad, mad," she sniffed.

"No, Mama's not mad." She shot a look at Mick. "Not at you. Come here." He bent so she could take the child from his shoulders.

"I'm sure this involves those kids, Ricky and Stephano," she said, while swaying side to side with Junie. "They had a score to settle, especially Stephano after I harassed him at work. They pried the back bedroom window open." She cuddled Junie. "Oh, Junie." She sighed. "This isn't how I imagined your homecoming would be."

"Where are the towels? I'll dry the hardwood."

"No, Mick. I told you..."

He stared her down. "Yes, I heard. No room in your life for anyone. You're mad at me for prying into your life and sending money. Got it. I'm going to dry the floor while you hold Junie. That's not prying or bossing, it's just salvaging."

Her eyes still sparked with fire that ignited something deep in his belly.

"Top shelf, hall closet," she said, voice cold.

Grateful that he could still be of some small service, he set off, boots squelching on the wet floor.

Was the house flood the work of two disgruntled teens? He wanted to believe it, but his gut told him it was something else, something far more sinister.

SEVENTEEN

When the kitchen floor was relatively dry, Keeley set June at the table with a tub of plastic animals to keep her occupied. Her mind spun with the latest setback. She did not have the money to replace carpets or the ruined draperies. Insurance would cover some, but she didn't even want to think about the deductible. Mick's thousand dollars would help, but she would not consider taking it. Her pride stung to think that all these months she'd been his charity case, a way to assuage his guilt. More than that, she'd let herself grow fond of him, a man who saw her as a duty, someone who needed a caretaker.

She brushed away the thoughts. The first problem at hand was what to do with Junie. The only bedroom was unlivable, at least until she got the sodden carpet removed. Aunt Viv would of course welcome Junie again, but Keeley hated to ask. She was supposed to be the mother, the provider, and it was time to stop taking advantage of Aunt Viv. John had an extra bedroom and he'd like nothing better than for them to come and stay with him, but Mick's accusation stuck in her mind. John's attention had always elicited an odd feeling in Keeley, but she knew he would never stoop to damaging her home in order to convince her to stay with him. Would he?

"This is ridiculous. I know John. Mick doesn't." She snatched up her cell phone and dialed John's number.

"Hi, John, it's Keeley."

"Is something wrong? You sound tense."

Wrong? Everything was wrong. She should go stay with the man and let him provide a dry place for her daughter, for goodness' sake. It would be so easy. "Um, no. Nothing's wrong. I actually... Everything is fine. I'm not going to come in to help with the birds tonight. Something's come up."

"Are you sure you're okay? Do you need any help?"

"No, we're fine. I'll probably see you tomorrow."

"Okay," he said doubtfully. "But I'm here if you need anything, remember that."

She disconnected. Had it come to this? That she did not trust anyone? She'd wanted so badly to shut everyone out after LeeAnn's death, to prove to herself that she did not need to let anyone in as she assumed the role of a mother figure. It had been easy to do, until Mick arrived on the scene.

You don't need him. You can do this all by yourself. God's equipped you, remember?

Mick dumped a pile of wet towels in the corner of the kitchen. "I pulled up the carpet in the bedroom and put cardboard over the nails. Hallway and bathroom are dry. Windows are open to dry things out." He hesitated. "Will you hear out a suggestion?"

She nodded for him to continue.

"You and June sleep in the camper tonight, since it will be cold with all the windows open."

She felt miserable. Of course Mick would no longer need to stay in the camper. His job was done now that Tucker was caught. The only bright spot was that she could have Junie with her overnight, finally, if she could find a spot dry enough.

"Okay," she said dully. "She has a playdate today. That will give me some time to contact the flooring people and the insurance company."

The silence grew awkward between them.

"Please thank your father again for his kindness when you get back," she said.

"Okay."

"Why do I get the sense you're not leaving right away?" She ignored the hopeful feeling that sprang up inside her.

"Got loose ends to nail down."

"What?"

He didn't answer.

"You're going to check out the rooftop."

Still no answer.

"Because you think Tucker might be innocent after all."

"Because I still don't know why he was interested in staying on that rooftop. That's all."

"I'm going, too."

"No."

"You don't get to tell me what to do. If Tucker is innocent, then someone else killed my sister."

"And if it is someone else, they're not going to want you to find out. That puts you in danger."

"It's my call, not yours." She paused. "Soon you'll be out of here and I'll be left to raise my sister's child. Someday I want to tell Junie when she's old enough that the bad person, whoever that is, was held responsible for what he did to her mother."

"I want that for you, too."

She added quietly, "That's the only way you'll ever be free of the guilt…and me." She'd expected to find hardness in his eyes, the flinty soldier whom she'd taken to task, the overbearing guy who'd interfered. Instead she found softness there in his chocolate gaze, a shimmering sweetness as he stared at her that made her knees weak.

Slowly, he reached up his hand and traced one finger along the side of her face. "Keeley," he said. "I'll never get you out of my heart." Then he turned and walked out.

I'll never get you out of my heart. Had he really said that? Given voice to the strange longing that had nested deep inside him? It was true. After he'd gone home, back to the quiet sanctuary with his father and his birds, she would remain in his soul, if only in his memory. Mick was not a person of great imagination, but he'd often found himself wondering what life would have been like if his son had lived. He knew his mind would harbor similar musings about Keeley. Their lives would be separate, but his heart would drift back to her. Why? Was it guilt? He did not think so, not anymore. Was it love, then?

It could not be that. She would not allow it, and with good reason. He'd barreled his way in uninvited, and he above all people had the least right to do so. Keeley's focus was June, as it should be, and she wanted no one else involved. Enough said. He drove to Reggie's place.

Reggie was outside, polishing his old 1971 Mustang, from the windshield wipers to the personalized plates and everything in between. The sheen off the red paint glowed like hot coals.

"Thought you'd show up here sooner or later." He wiped his hands on a rag. "Finally got Rivendale. I'm just sorry it wasn't me that shot him."

"He's still alive."

Reggie shrugged. "Docs say he's in a coma. Most likely won't make it. Save a lot of effort if he didn't."

The skin around Reggie's good eye was pinched, stubble showed on his normally clean-shaven chin.

Things hadn't gone well with the cops, probably. Best to be direct. "Why didn't you say that Bruce was your parolee?"

"Well," he said, heaving out a deep breath, "cops already grilled me. I guess it's only fair that you have your turn."

Mick waited.

"Fact is, Mick, I didn't remember."

Mick couldn't conceal his disbelief. "Come on. You're the guy who remembers ever collar you ever made in your thirty-year cop career. You memorize baseball stats like nobody's business. Don't tell me you forgot a guy like Bruce."

"See, that's where it gets a little embarrassing for me. I haven't been as meticulous as I should have with my cases. I might have been a tad careless."

Mick was getting a sinking feeling in his gut. "How careless?"

"Come on, Mick. You know these parolees. Some are heavy-duty and some are the lightweights. I sort of rubber-stamped a few of the minor offenders."

"Rubber-stamped?"

He shrugged. "You know, wrote up some notes, passed them along through the system without really doing too much checking."

Mick groaned. "I can't be hearing this right."

He shrugged. "Got so many cases, who can really pay attention to them all? You know what the workload is like. Upward of one hundred ten cases at any given time."

"So you dummied the paperwork?"

"That sounds harsh."

"It is harsh," Mick snapped. "You made up things? Job interviews? Drug test results? All of it?"

"Only for a few, and not the real bad boys. One two-bit criminal doesn't make a difference."

"Only this one might have, Reg. This one might have been working with Tucker Rivendale." He tried to bring his volume down without success. "This one might have killed a girl."

He looked away. "What I hear, she was a parolee, too."

"That doesn't mean she deserved to die."

"Of course not, and don't put words in my mouth." He was angry now. "LeeAnn Stevens didn't deserve to die, either. That's why I came here in the first place, to deal with Tucker Rivendale, a guy who killed a girl, too, and on your watch, I might add, so maybe you can knock off the high-and-mighty gimmick."

They stood in silence for a moment, Mick breathing hard, trying to rein in his temper. Finally he nodded. "Okay. I guess we're both in damage-control mode."

"Aside from the fact that I'm probably going to be forced into early retirement or fired, the damage is controlled. Rivendale is neutralized and the cops will watch out for the brothers."

Mick nodded.

"But you're not convinced about something." Reggie shook his head. "Please don't tell me you think Tucker is innocent."

"I need to check out the rooftop. Find out what he was after."

Reggie laughed, a bitter sound. "I didn't do my job, and you can't stop doing yours. Ironic."

"Yeah, ironic."

"For what it's worth, you were a good parole officer, Mick. You'd still be one, if you'd ease up on yourself."

"I'm hearing that a lot lately."

"Keeley bending your ear?" He offered a sly smile.

"I'm leaving as soon as I can, Reg."

He sighed. "Just as well. Women are nothing but trouble. Nadine loves horses, and you know how much those cost? Why can't she adore a nice poodle? Something that doesn't require a stable and a saddle."

Mick smiled in spite of himself.

"Anyway, I'm not gonna ask your forgiveness for cutting corners because I don't really care if you forgive me or not. That's my trouble, I guess. Don't care."

"You care about Nadine."

"Yeah," he said softly. "I guess she's the one person who made it through my tough-guy defenses."

Reggie arched an eyebrow. "Could be Keeley's that one girl who makes it through yours."

"No."

"Okay. I'm just thinking that having a woman love you and a family to go home to at night beats scouring filthy rooftops in search of evidence to prove you weren't wrong." He turned back to the car. "Catch you later, maybe."

Mick turned back to the truck and drove back to Silver Creek.

The sun appeared and disappeared between clouds, dappling him with light and shadow as he drove. How many miles had he covered in the past year and a half? Traveling roads of self-recrimination and loathing, trapped and steeped in guilt? He'd been blind to Reggie's transgressions, blind to the people who had tried to come alongside him and offer him solace. Imprisoned.

Keeley's words came back to him. *God forgives everything because you're His son.*

"Lord," he said aloud. "If You're listening, I'm sorry. For everything. If You'll forgive me for my heap of sins—" He found his eyes were damp. "I'll try to forgive myself."

He did not feel a bolt of energy or the sudden wash of contentment, but something inside him eased just a fraction, a corner of the darkness lifted and Mick knew, in that moment, that God was with him.

On a lonely country road.

In a beat-up old Ford.

He took up the key God offered and let himself out of the prison.

Keeley drove June to five-year-old Bonnie's house in Big Pines. It was one of Junie's favorite things of all time to spend the afternoon with her friend Bonnie, and Keeley was grateful that LeeAnn had struck up a friendship with Bonnie's mom, Roberta. Bonnie, too, had Down syndrome, and the girls had bonded at various playgroups and in doctors' waiting rooms. After LeeAnn's death, Roberta had stepped right in to make sure that June and Bonnie had playtime together. Keeley learned so much from Roberta, an experienced mother of four—everything from where to buy musical toothbrushes to how to administer a proper time-out for misbehavior.

Roberta greeted them both with warm hugs and an offer of coffee for Keeley.

"We're hoping to go to the movies this afternoon. Is it okay to keep her for a while?"

Keeley agreed, thanking Roberta and reaching for her wallet.

"My treat," Roberta said, stopping her.

Keeley's cheeks burned as she accepted the offer. Roberta was aware that money was tight. What would she think if she knew the condition of Keeley's sodden carpets and ruined curtains? Clamping down on a measure of despair, Keeley departed.

After a quick stop at home and several maddening phone calls to the insurance company, she once again took her place in the passenger seat of Mick's truck. *One more time, that's all*, she told herself. She avoided looking at his strong profile, keeping her gaze fastened out the window. *Get it over with. Quick.*

When the panic started to rise inside, she said some silent prayers. *Help me do this, God. If Tucker's innocent, help me find out. Help me be enough. Junie needs me.*

And who do you need? The question rumbled through her mind. No one. Now that Tucker was in custody, her obstacle was overcome. She and Junie were safe and no longer needed the police, or John, or Mick Hudson. Why, then, did her body seem to yearn for Mick's gentle embrace? She clenched her hands into balls to keep herself from remembering the feel of his rough hands as he held hers; every tender glance, each gentle word he'd spoken to Junie nestled down inside Keeley like a newly fledged bird. Even the shame and anger over his anonymous checks had subsided. Why had God drawn Mick, the least likely person that should comfort her, into their lives?

You don't need him, she told herself.

But did she?

Keeley bit her lip. It didn't matter anyway. He would be gone right after their rooftop excursion.

Gone, and Keeley would be ready to resume her life again. The thought left her flat and cold inside.

They pulled up at the newspaper building to find it had been securely locked.

"Looks as if it's the fire escape again," she said as she sighed. Memories of meeting Tucker and the sound of whistling bullets made her skin erupt in prickles, but she dutifully followed Mick up the ladders until they reached the top.

The afternoon sunshine finally beat back the clouds and she blinked against the sheen of the concrete. On the rooftop below, the colony of Quaker parrots bustled about, preening and tending to their tangle of nests. She remembered the green feather. "There's a man, his name is Meeker. He studies and films the parrot colonies. I think he's writing a book about them."

Mick didn't answer. She turned to find him down on one knee, surveying. "Tucker's diagram was accurate. There's the electrical box and the ventilation vents."

"And the air-conditioning unit. But why'd he bother? What could be here that he was looking for?"

"LeeAnn came here to tend to an injured bird, right?"

"Yes, but there was blood in the parking lot, which is where she was probably killed. There was no sign she even climbed up according to the police."

"But what if she did? What if she saw something? Got proof of something?"

Keeley's breath hitched. "She sent me that one text telling me she was in trouble. Maybe she took a picture, too."

Mick looked at her. "Did they ever find her phone?"

"No."

"Okay. So if she took a picture and dropped her phone after she sent the text to you, where could it have fallen?"

They spent the next forty-five minutes trying to answer the question, moving the pallets, scouring every dirty corner of the rooftop with no success.

Keeley finally collapsed to her knees on the cement. "This is ridiculous," she said.

"Maybe I was wrong. Wouldn't be the first time." Mick rubbed a hand over his eyes. "I'm sorry if I gave you false hope that we'd find something."

Keeley sighed. A little puff of feathers bumped across the rooftop, nudged along by a spring breeze. She watched the bit of fluff tumble along, catching for a moment on the bottom edge of the air-conditioning unit before it was blown underneath. "That's it." Keeley scrambled over to the unit and laid down flat on her stomach.

Mick followed suit, grunting in frustration. "I'm too big to get close. What's in there?"

"I'm not sure." She slid her hand into the gap, pushing through dirty feathers and dry leaves, hoping she wasn't about to have a close encounter with a rodent. Finally her fingers closed around a hard rectangular object, and she pulled it free.

They both stared at the pink plastic case.

LeeAnn's phone.

EIGHTEEN

Keeley's hand shook as she pressed the phone, cracked screen and all, to her cheek. It felt both wonderful and terrible to feel it there, knowing the last person to hold it had been her precious sister right before her life was ripped away. The tears rolled unchecked, and the grief swelled so big she thought it would tear her apart. All the anguish that she'd thought had ebbed came back in one excruciating rush.

Mick pulled her to her feet and cradled her in his arms. He didn't say a word. She didn't need him to. In that moment of overwhelming emotion, she accepted the comfort and tenderness, the simple gesture from a complex man, the gentle touch of a battle-scarred soldier. He pressed his lips to her forehead, her temples and grazed her cheek. "I'm sorry this hurts."

She breathed hard, in and out, trying to pull herself away, and not finding the strength. It trickled into her soul slowly, like a fresh stream fed by spring rains. God did not want her to be alone in her grief, and He'd put Mick in her life, in that moment, to share the burden with her. She returned the embrace, circling his wide shoulders and burying her face in the slow and steady beat of his heart.

When her crying slowed, he eased her away, bending to look her in the eye.

"Are you okay?"

She nodded, returning her attention once more to the phone. "It's dead. No charge."

"I have a charger cord in my truck. Do you… Are you able to climb down?"

She wiped her cheeks with the back of her sleeve. "Yes."

"All right. Let's go see if this phone will help us find answers."

She thought with a lurch that the answers would mean Mick would be free to be on his way. Of course. What other alternative was there? God had put Mick into her life, but it didn't mean he was meant to stay there. *And that's the way I want it,* she told herself.

They made it down and into the truck. Mick started the engine and plugged the charger cord into the phone. She found herself clutching his hand, breath held, to see if there would be any sign of life from the battered cell.

A light flicked to life, and the home screen showed hazily through the web of cracks. Keeley fought another wave of agony as LeeAnn's screen saver, a picture of Junie flashing a gummy infant grin, sprang to life. She pressed the photos icon, Mick's arm tight around her. Together they peered at the tiny images. There were only two from the rooftop. One was a close-up of a Quaker parrot, fluffed and limp winged, perched on the edge of the concrete roof.

Mick pointed. "What's he got on him?"

Keeley's pulse hammered both from the photo and the muscled arm caging her. "It's a little device." She squinted. "A camera, I think."

Mick's breath hitched. "You said there was a man who was filming the bird colony."

She nodded. "Webb Meeker. Hang on. There's one more photo after that."

The other picture caught only the edge of the ventilation shaft and a blurry shot of Tucker Rivendale.

Liar. He'd been there. He'd killed LeeAnn after all. "He was on the rooftop that day." Keeley's head whirled. "I don't get it. Did he kill her when they climbed back down? Why climb up at all if he was that angry with her?"

Mick pointed to the edge of the picture. "There. That's somebody's shoulder. A man's, by the look of it. Tucker was on that rooftop with someone else, and LeeAnn caught them on film. Maybe that's why he killed her."

"Or the other person killed her and Tucker was telling the truth."

Suddenly a shadow edged into her peripheral vision. She did not have time to scream before the windshield exploded as Bruce swung a bat at the passenger-side glass. It took him another vicious swing to smash completely through, sending tiny bits of cubed glass swirling around the truck.

Bruce reached in and opened the door, dragging Keeley from the car.

Charlie went for Mick, but she could not see clearly through the flying glass as Bruce hauled her to the ground, yanking her wrist so hard she thought it would snap. She screamed and kicked, but his hold did not loosen until he flung her to the ground, driving the breath out of her while he wrestled the phone from her death grip.

He grinned. "Thought we'd left town?"

"You killed Ginny. Why?" she panted as he moved close, the bat still in one hand, the phone shoved in his pocket.

"We were schooling her, but it got out of hand. An accident."

An accident. Ginny was a young, vulnerable girl, like LeeAnn had been. "And my sister?"

Bruce came closer. "Don't know your sister. Don't care."

Don't care.

The words chased each other around inside, cutting and burning, igniting rage inside her like a white-hot flame. He gripped the bat, twisting his

arms in preparation for the swing that would probably kill her.

No, you won't.

When he weighted back, she kicked with all her
might, taking his legs out from under him. He went
over backward with a grunt of surprise. She leaped
up. Mick was just rounding the front of the truck,
Charlie on the ground behind him, stunned.

Bruce was already scrambling to his feet, so
Keeley did not need Mick to tell her what to do.
Grabbing hands, they ran to the truck, and Mick hit
the gas, grit spraying off the tires. Bruce appeared
at the driver's door, wrenching it open.

Mick leveled a punch that connected with Bruce's
temple, driving him back until he lost his grip.

Mick sent the truck shooting forward, only taking a moment to reach out and close the driver's
door. Keeley was panting, her body too shaken to
register much but the fact that they had escaped.

Mick clutched her fingers. "Did he hurt you?"

"No," she managed to reply, trying to calm her
rasping breaths. "I think they killed Ginny. To
teach her a lesson of some kind. He said he didn't
know my sister."

"Could be lying, but even if he isn't, there was
someone on the roof with Tucker, and that person
has a connection to the psycho brothers. Could have
even been them up there with Tucker that day."

She groaned. "Bruce has the cell phone. Now
we're back to having no proof again."

"There might be proof. There was a camera on that bird."

She nodded. "If Meeker was recording the life of the colony with the bird cams, he might have gotten something on tape. He's got a shop in Big Pines, I think. It's a long shot."

"Better than no shot."

He handed her his phone. "Call the police. Ask for Chief Allen." He shook his head, seemingly talking to himself. "I should have seen it coming with Charlie and Bruce. Should have seen things going south with Reggie."

"Is Reggie involved?"

"He was Bruce's parole officer, but he's been faking the supervision, or so he says."

"You don't trust him anymore?"

Mick didn't answer for a long moment. "I'm not going to trust anyone until this is all wrapped up. We're going to find Meeker, and if that doesn't pan out, I will spend every waking moment tracking Bruce and Charlie with or without the police, or Reggie, or anybody else, and not out of guilt, either." He flicked her a glance. "Been praying about it."

Her heart lifted, a warm golden glow filling her. "You're on speaking terms again?"

"Oh, He's never stopped speaking, I just wasn't listening. I—I think I found my soul again."

She took his hand, and he pulled her carefully into the circle of his arm. He didn't elaborate, but she knew there was something profoundly changed about him; the heavy stain of guilt was lifted from his brown eyes. They were now filled with a clean, clear determination.

"I'm going to finish this," he said. "Before I go."

Before I go. She swallowed hard. The fire burning in his eyes was not for her, and she wasn't sure why she had expected anything else.

He had a mission to complete, a case to close.

No other reason to stay.

She'd just finished up her call with the police when her phone rang.

"Hey, honey. I'm going to bring Cornelius home from his wing-and-nail grooming and then I'm craving a walk to the park. Would Junie like to come along?"

Keeley explained calmly what had happened and where they were headed. "Junie's at Roberta's until five. If I'm not back by then, can you get Junie?"

"Yes, but, Keeley, this sounds dangerous. I wish I could ask Derek what he thinks we should do, but…" She sighed. "He's not taking my calls. I don't know where he is."

Keeley understood. Ginny was dead, and he was suspended from duty. She made a mental note to pray for Chief Uttley. "I'm sorry about all of it, Aunt Viv."

"Me, too," she said. "My heart's a little bit broken right now." She disconnected.

A little bit broken. Ginny dead, Tucker clinging to life, and then there was Mick. She resisted the urge to look at him—the strong chin and dark hair, the lines that had been carved into his face by love and loss.

Before I go.

Remember, Keeley, she told herself. *You're going to be alone again in a matter of days. You're going to be all right.* She sneaked one quick look at his mouth, full lips clamped into a determined line.

She pulled her gaze away and fixed her eyes out the front windshield, just as determined as Mick to see their mission completed.

Meeker's place was an old one-story cabin set at the top of a gravel road. The tires threw rocks against the undercarriage, which Mick heard clearly, since the passenger-side window glass was gone. If he'd had his choice he would have driven Keeley back to her aunt Viv's. Bruce had come close, too close, to hurting her. He wished he could count on Reggie or even Uttley to provide backup, but he was beyond asking for help from anyone. A sense of urgency hammered away at his insides. The longer the situation continued, the more at risk Keeley became.

He parked the truck and they knocked on the front door. No one answered, so he pounded louder.

"Mr. Meeker?" Keeley called. "We need to talk to you about one of your parrots."

Silence.

"Please, Mr. Meeker. It's urgent," she added.

Feet shuffled to the door and it opened a few inches. A man in his fifties with a shaggy puff of hair regarded them warily.

"What do you want?"

Keeley smiled and Mick stepped back a pace, figuring his presence was probably spooking the guy.

"My sister took a picture of one of your birds almost two years ago. It looked as if the bird had a camera strapped to its body and we figure it's yours. Did you recover the camera, Mr. Meeker? Do you remember?"

"Maybe."

"My sister was killed. We think your camera might have captured the image of her killer." Keeley held up her hands. "Please, Mr. Meeker. My sister was a bird lover and she went to a rooftop to help one of your parrots. Do you know anything that would shed light on her murder?"

He answered by flinging the door open and retreating into the house. Mick followed him, Keeley right behind. They made their way through a hallway cluttered with books and into a tiny living room crammed with computers, more bird books and piles of papers.

"My fault," Meeker said. "Bird got herself caught on a fence because of the camera. I check on them every few days, but I didn't know that particular female was injured until I trapped her to remove the camera. Had to wait until the cops let me into the parking lot. By then the poor thing was nearly dead."

"So you did retrieve the camera?" Keeley's face burned with hope.

"Course I did. I'm working on a documentary about the Quaker colony." His face softened. "Got hours of footage. Even got a tiny camera in one of their nesting holes. That mama bird hatched eight eggs after I fixed her up, and all of them survived."

"Please can we see the footage you got from that camera, Mr. Meeker? It's vitally important," Keeley said.

Meeker's eyes narrowed. "It's my property."

"We don't want to take your property. We'd just like to see it."

This was taking too long. Mick straightened, staring down at the much shorter man. "You can show us, or we can get the police here and you can show them."

Meeker sat down on a rolling office chair and tapped his computer to life. "All right. You can look. Here's the footage."

Meeker did not offer them a chair, so he and Keeley stood behind and watched over his shoulder. The video was jerky, capturing the little bird's journey as she took off from the communal nest to forage in the forest. She encountered several other members of her colony eating seeds on the forest floor. When she landed on a barbed wire fence, Meeker grimaced. Mick did, too, as she became caught, struggling to free herself with a frantic flapping of her wings. Finally loose, her flight became less controlled.

"Got a terrible cut on her wing, you see," Meeker said. "And she was exhausted from her escape. She couldn't make it back to the nest right away, so she stopped to rest on the newspaper building."

Keeley hugged herself as the footage showed the familiar rooftop.

There was no sound, only the drab cement roof. The camera lens was fixed on the side of a ventilation shaft. Two minutes passed, then three. The bird suddenly rustled to life and took off over the side of the roof, capturing a few seconds of the parking lot below, and then it went black.

"Batteries quit." Meeker sat back. "Got what you wanted?"

"No."

Mick heard the desperate disappointment in her voice.

"The camera didn't show anyone on the rooftop. Not even Tucker." Her voice broke.

"Can we rewind about fifteen seconds?" Mick asked.

Meeker took the video back and played it again.

"There," Mick said. "Stop it there."

He froze the picture.

"It's Tucker's car," Keeley said. "But that doesn't help. We already knew he was there."

Mick's heart turned to stone.

"In front of it," he said, forcing out the words.

She leaned closer. "It's the trunk of another car. The first three letters of the license plate are *L*, *V*, *N*..."

"It says LVNADIE."

"How do you know that?"

"It's short for 'love Nadine', Reggie's pet name for his wife."

"Reggie Donaldson? Your colleague? That's his car."

The pieces fell into place. "He was doing some kind of business with Tucker on the rooftop. He didn't want Tucker caught, he wanted him dead."

"Yes and no," Reggie said, stepping into the room and locking the door behind him.

NINETEEN

Mick was sickened, staring at the man he'd once respected.

"Lucky thing that Charlie and Bruce were able to tell me in which direction you were headed. I'm a little rusty at tailing people."

"I thought you were one of the good guys."

"That's your problem—always black-and-white. I am a good guy, but I needed money, Mick, pure and simple. Tucker had connections, so I pressured him to steal cars for me and deliver them to a chop shop. Told him if he didn't, I'd cook up some evidence to have him arrested on some charge or another."

"The Quick Stop Garage," Keeley said. "Charlie and Bruce. They're your partners."

"Yeah, and it went fine until Tucker wanted out. He was gonna go to the cops regardless of my threats. We met on the rooftop and I lost my temper. Your sister appeared just as I knocked Tucker out."

He grinned. "Might have even loosened a tooth on that pretty face of his."

"That's why LeeAnn called. She wasn't afraid of Tucker, she was afraid *for* him. You killed my sister," Keeley hissed.

"That's where the 'no' part comes in. She scurried back down the fire escape. I lugged Tucker down the inside stairs and when I got to the parking lot, there was no sign of her. I was gonna put Tucker in my trunk, but he came to and broke away. Took off in his car and I took off after him. Crashed into the pond, and believe me there was no one more surprised than I was when they popped that trunk and LeeAnn was inside."

Mick grunted. "That's not even close to a credible story. I would have thought you'd come up with something more convincing."

"Yeah, I know. Who killed LeeAnn while I was busy lugging Tucker down the stairs? I've wondered that for a good long time now." He shrugged. "Anyway, I was happy to let everyone think Tucker did it. He went on the run and I encouraged Ginny to make contact. She'd been friends with Tucker back in the day and she was working at Bruce and Charlie's garage, so it seemed like the perfect idea."

"How exactly did you encourage her?" Mick said, not bothering to hide the sarcasm.

"She was into drugs. It was an easy choice for her. Do what I ask or I turn you in."

"So she contacted Tucker on your behalf, without him knowing you were pulling the strings," Keeley said.

"It was easy. She was already his friend, so she strung him along until he trusted her completely. I had her tell him that he was Junie's father when I found out a few months back, knowing he'd come to see her."

"So you could kill him."

"It was gonna be great," he said with a sigh. "I sent Keeley a text to get her on that rooftop, and I was going to be the big hero and kill Tucker right there with you as a witness, Mick. Tucker isn't worth a plug nickel. Would have been so much better if my plan worked out."

Acid burned inside Mick. "And was Ginny's life worthless, too?"

"I sure didn't tell Bruce and Charlie to kill that girl. I asked them to scare her a little, since she was going to tell Tucker that I was planning an ambush for him. Had the dumb idea she could enlist the help of the stalwart Hudson family. I couldn't let that go. Bruce and Charlie went overboard with the convincing, and they left for a while."

"Until you sent them to make sure I didn't find anything on the rooftop."

"When you told me about Tucker's diagram, I knew there was something on that roof. I figured she must have dropped a phone or a camera or something and he was after it to prove I was on that rooftop. Should have been over when Uttley took Tucker out, but you just couldn't let it go, could you?"

"No, I guess not."

"You'd take the word of a dirty car thief over mine."

Mick almost laughed. "Over a lying blackmailer? Any day."

Reggie's eyebrows knitted into an angry line. "You marine types. All spit and polish and honor. Well, you know what? That's not the real world. The real world is bills and vermin who get off parole and continue to be vermin and wives who fall out of love with you."

"Maybe," Mick said quietly, "she fell out of love with you because you turned into a person she didn't respect anymore."

He nodded, shoulders slouched as if the anger had drained out of him. "You're probably right, but I'm in too deep now. I wouldn't do well in prison." He pulled a gun from his pocket.

Meeker whimpered.

"You should have listened to me about carrying a weapon, Mick. Now all three of you are going to have to pay the price. I feel bad about that. I really do."

Keeley felt her whole body go ice-cold. Meeker stood.

"Are going to kill us?" Meeker whispered.

Meeker looked so terrified that Keeley wanted

to soothe him, but she could think of nothing to say. Reggie was going to murder them. That much was clear. She reached slowly for the cell phone in her pocket.

"No," Reggie said. "No calls."

Mick stood tall, huge in the cluttered room. He edged over a few inches to shield her and Meeker.

"Reggie, listen. This is between you and me. Those two are just bystanders. They're going to leave here, and you're going to let them go because you're not a cold-blooded killer."

He smiled. "And they're never going to contact the police or play that bird video for the cops, right? Not buying that one." He looked at Keeley. "You know, for what it's worth, I really was torn up about seeing your sister dead there in that trunk. I didn't kill her and I don't know who did, but now I've got to kill you. Blood on my hands after all."

Keeley could not look at him. Her eyes were fixed on the round barrel of the gun, which seemed enormous.

"It's not gonna be like that, Reg," Mick said, taking another sideways step. "You're not going to kill those two."

Meeker groaned. "This isn't happening."

Keeley knew the only thing she could do was make a break for the door to unlock it. At least Meeker might be able to escape. He could go the police and tell them everything. She eyed the bolt, a simple twist and turn. It would take her only three seconds, but three seconds was less time than it would take for Reggie to shoot her in the back. And Mick…

Her eyes soaked in his strong profile, the courage that made him stand straight, chin up, shoulders lifted.

I think I found my soul again.

He'd never really lost it, she thought. It had just been buried under layers of guilt. Now he was free to live the life God intended for him, or give it up trying to save her.

No. It could not happen, and what's more she wasn't about to let Junie lose the only mother she had left. She scanned the room, looking for something with which to distract Reggie. There was nothing, only piles of yellowed paper.

"Meeker has the videos saved on a hard drive. It's in his safety deposit box," she blurted out.

Reggie raised an eyebrow. "Nice try, but I'm thinking Meeker here isn't the type to arrange for that sort of thing. I'm thinking he's the kind of guy who keeps his money stuffed in a mattress. In any case, I'm willing to take that risk."

She heard it, then, the sound that just might save them. "Someone is coming."

He sighed. "I gotta give you credit for persistence. That's enough…" He broke off suddenly as the sound of an engine rumbled to life.

They both seized the moment. Mick lunged for

Reggie's gun arm and Keeley threw herself at the door, flinging it open.

"Run," she shouted to Meeker.

He sprinted out.

She turned her attention back to Mick who was wrestling Reggie. The gun fired and she dived to the floor as the bullet shattered the window. Terror for Mick made her raise her head again to see Mick smashing Reggie's gun hand against the floor.

Reggie's face was red with exertion, one hand wrapped around Mick's throat. Mick was stronger, his muscles bunched with effort, sweat beading his forehead as he forced Reggie to release his grip on the gun.

Keeley scrambled over and grabbed it.

Mick was panting hard, eyes locked on Reggie, who went limp in defeat.

The front door banged and Derek Uttley burst in, gun drawn, eyes taking in every detail. "Seems as though you have it handled, Mr. Hudson."

Mick heaved himself to his feet and took the gun from Keeley, putting it on a table in the corner.

Uttley continued to keep the gun trained on Reggie. "Since I'm suspended, I got lots of time. Found a journal at Ginny's place and it told all about you. Viv said you two were headed up here and I figured I'd tag along. Glad I did." He knelt closer, hatred blazing across his face. "It'd save the justice system a lot of time if I just kill you here."

Keeley's stomach lurched and Mick moved closer.

"No, Chief," Mick said.

"Not a chief anymore. I have no job and Ginny..." His voice broke. "I felt a little bit like her dad, so now I have no kid, either, thanks to this piece of trash."

"You'll get your job back," Keeley said, watching his finger tighten on the trigger. "Please don't do this."

Uttley grimaced. "She was just a kid."

Mick put a hand on Uttley's shoulder. "Listen to me. Reggie is a parole officer. There's nothing worse you can do to him than send him to jail with the people he despises most."

Uttley's mouth twitched, and after an endless moment, he lowered his weapon.

Keeley let out a breath.

Reggie looked up at Mick, face puzzled. "I don't belong with those criminals and you know it."

Mick shrugged. "Sometimes there is justice in this world," he said.

Keeley refused with all the strength left in her to go to the police station. "I'm going to get my daughter," she told Uttley and Mick, "and if anyone wants to talk to me before tomorrow morning, they can show up at my house."

Mick didn't argue, but she caught a glimmer of a smile on his face as he drove her to Aunt Viv's at a maddeningly slow pace. She wanted to give voice to all the feelings tumbling around inside her, but she didn't dare. She needed time to sort it out. The memory of Mick putting his body between her and a gun for the second time would not leave her mind. She did not want to talk about Reggie's strange confession or their harrowing escape. Most of all, she did not want to hear Mick say goodbye.

Junie was in the playroom banging blocks around. Keeley kissed and hugged her until the little girl squirmed to be free. Keeley left her to play and told Aunt Viv everything that had transpired.

Viv clutched her close, tears running down her cheeks. "Oh, Keeley. Oh, honey." She released Keeley and wrapped a startled Mick in a hug.

"Thank you for protecting her," she sobbed.

Mick looked strained. "Ah, it was a joint effort, ma'am. Keeley had a hand in it, too." He patted her back awkwardly and immediately escaped into the playroom when she released him.

Viv collapsed onto the sofa. "I got a text from Derek. He wants to talk. I think that's progress, don't you?"

She did. "He's got a lot to work through, and there's no better listener than you, Aunt Viv."

She sighed. "I'll get Junie's bag."

While she was gone, Keeley found Mick and Junie collaborating over a block tower on the floor. Mick was on his stomach, long frame sprawling.

Angry that her tower had collapsed once again, Junie threw her block to the floor, cheeks red. "No, no," she shouted.

"Like this," Mick said. He put four blocks together to form a sturdy base for the tower. "Now try."

Junie did, ferociously determined to control her finger muscles. With the more stable platform, she managed to stack four blocks atop the structure.

Mick nodded. "There you go. Now you can knock it down."

Junie did, this time squealing with delight as the blocks tumbled everywhere. She went to chase them and Mick laughed. He found Keeley staring at him.

"She just needed a different way to do it."

Keeley felt her throat swell. "I was crushed when we found out Junie had Down syndrome. I fixated on the things she wouldn't be able to do. I thought it was some sort of punishment, but I've figured out it's just the way God meant her to be."

"She's pretty great just the way she is."

"Yes." She paused. "You'll be a great dad someday, Mick."

He flushed and looked away. "Not sure about that. Figured I wasn't meant to have kids, not after my son."

"And I figured I wasn't going to be a mother, until Junie."

He watched Junie, a wistful look washing over his face. "Funny how God puts you places you'd never choose to go."

"Yes, funny," she said, gathering June into her

arms. The girl wriggled, stretching out her arms to Mick.

"Up."

His eyes widened. "Oh, up like on my shoulders? I think she remembers from before."

"It's okay if you don't want to," Keeley said.

He looked from Keeley to the little hands out-stretched to him. Then he took June up and swung her onto his shoulders.

"Yeah, yeah," Junie called, her face wreathed in a smile.

Mick grinned, bending to whisper to Keeley, "You don't think she'll make me sing again, do you?"

Keeley laughed. "Just remember, you're the grown-up. You can tell her no."

He raised a skeptical eyebrow, which set Keeley laughing again.

Mick trotted her outside with plenty of extra bouncing. Junie was thrilled.

Keeley watched them, her heart both happy and broken.

How sweet a moment.

And how unutterably sad that it would be their last together.

The drive back to her house was quiet.

Junie ran ahead when they got there, Keeley opened the door and let her inside. She lingered on the porch.

"Are you going back home after the police are done with you?" she forced herself to say.

"I guess so." He studied her, his gaze drifting from her hair to her eyes to her lips. "There are some ends to tie up, and I'm going to stop and see Tucker before I go, if he regains consciousness. I have a feeling that he thought I knew about Reggie's blackmail, maybe that I was even in on it somehow. That's why he didn't come to me for help." He sighed.

The sunlight silhouetted his strong frame, the long arms that she ached to feel around her. But what right had she to ask him to stay? She was a woman with a child to raise, and he had come for one purpose only.

"Keeley—" He broke off.

"Yes?"

He shook his head. "Never mind. Everything's happened so fast I'm running off at the mouth. I just wanted to say that you're an amazing woman and an incredible mother." He reached down and caressed her arms, pressing his cheek to her temple, his lips grazing her brow. "I came here to save you, but I think it might have wound up the other way around."

She reveled in his warmth, the gentleness in his huge hands. *I don't want you to leave. Please stay here with me.*

Her heart squeezed out the words, but she could not speak them. He could not just stay out of duty;

he should remain out of love, and that had to come from him. After a long, bittersweet moment, he moved away.

"Say goodbye to June for me, will you?"

She nodded, unable to trust herself.

He walked to his truck and drove away.

With limbs made of iron, she dragged herself into the house and closed the door, leaning her forehead against the wood. Each breath was an agony.

"Good riddance" came a voice from behind her.

TWENTY

Mick drove.

Though the pace was his usual steady and slow, the miles brought no comfort.

The wheels churned up an ache inside him, an excruciating sense that he'd turned his back on a profound need. But the case was closed, Tucker would be exonerated of LeeAnn's murder, and for all Reggie's protestations, he'd more than likely murdered LeeAnn. The brothers would be charged with Ginny's death. So why the need pounding away at his insides?

Might it be his own? The sweetness of time spent with Keeley and June stuck to him like a fragrance. But his gut traveled back in time to LccAnn's murder, his misjudgment not of Tucker, but of Reggie.

Memories mixed together.

Reggie's twisted smile.

The bottomless blue of Keeley's eyes.

Watching Uttley gun down Tucker, the desperation in Tucker's outstretched hand.

Building that block tower and seeing the gleam of triumph in a child and the happiness he'd felt at being a part of her small success.

Old hurts, new joys, tragic losses and the feel of Keeley in his arms.

Every cell in his body wanted to turn the truck around.

He gripped the wheel. "Lord, I know You've forgiven me, but what if she can't? What if I take a risk and she walks away?"

What if?

What if the key to his happiness was right there, in that old house with the woman who duct-taped her bread machine and knew songs about wheels on buses?

Keeley.

"What should I do, God? What?" A rush of feeling he couldn't put a name to prickled along his skin, invading his mind and plowing through the dark places of the past.

U-turn.

He was driving back to Keeley's house, faster than the speed limit, borne along by something higher than himself.

Keeley turned slowly around.

John stood with his hands in his pockets.

She sucked in a breath, scanning the room for June. "What are you doing here?"

"You know what I'm doing here. I was with Aunt

Viv when you called her. She was picking up Cornelius. She told me you were on your way to Meeker's. I called her to follow up and she said you saw a video that showed the killer's car in the parking lot." He shook his head. "It's funny. To be found out by a bird."

Found out? "John, why did you let yourself into my house, and where's June?"

"I know where you keep the spare key. It's how I turned on the water."

Her heart thudded. "You flooded my house? Why would you do that?"

"Same reason I threw the Molotov through the window." He huffed. "You're so dumb sometimes. I wanted you and June to come stay with me, to get away from Mick. He's not good for you. Just like Tucker."

His voice seemed to come from a long way off, as if he was reciting a speech he'd written.

"John," she said steadily, "where is June?"

"I put her in the basement, just temporarily, while we talked."

She rushed for the basement door, but he kicked out and took her legs from under her, sending her to the floor. He pressed his knee to her back.

"We have to talk. I need you to understand that we're a family. You can't keep letting people get between us. First Tucker and now Mick. It's not right." His kneecap pressed into her spine.

"John, please."

"You should have seen through Tucker. I told you he was a crook. I tailed him forever, saw him go up on the rooftop every month like clockwork. Whatever he was doing up there was illegal, for sure. Drugs, I think. That's why I told you about the bird. Got the tip on the phone that there was a wounded parrot. I knew," he said, voice gone suddenly soft, reaching out a hand to stroke her hair. "I knew you would go and see him there, LeeAnn, and then you'd realize he was a crook."

Keeley was numb, disbelief freezing her senses. "You sent LeeAnn because Tucker would be there?"

"I sent you, honey," he said, crooning, "so you could learn the truth."

"I'm not LeeAnn," she cried out. "I'm Keeley."

His tone hardened. "And still, even after you saw Tucker doing something bad up there, you charged down the fire escape, and what was the first thing you said? The very first words out of your mouth?"

She didn't answer, stunned.

He put his face to her ear and whispered, "You said, 'Please, John. We have to get help for Tucker.'" His fist bunched in her hair, fingers ice-cold. "For Tucker, you said. Even after you knew he was a criminal. I proved it to you." With each word he tugged at her hair.

Tears pricked her eyes. It was time, past time, for the truth to come out. "And you got mad, when... when I said that."

"I lost my temper and shoved you. You hit your

head on the fender. I knew it was bad, real bad." He spoke right into her ear. She felt spittle on her cheek. "Oh, LeeAnn. I never meant it to happen, I was just so angry that you wouldn't see the truth about him."

"So you put her..." She swallowed. She'd humor him until she could get to June. "You put me in Tucker's trunk." To suffer and die all alone. Rage lit up her blood, but she would not indulge it. Not until her little girl was safe.

"Tucker is the bad guy in all this." He sniffed. "But you're here now and we can be a family. Doesn't matter how it happened. You, me and Junie. I have two plane tickets at the office. We'll go get them and fly away. To Mexico. No one will find us there. Doesn't that sound nice?"

Two. He wasn't intending to take June, daughter of a man he despised. She struggled for breath. *Lord, help me*, she prayed. "Let me up, John. You're hurting me."

"Of course, sweetheart." He eased off at once and reached out a hand to help her to her feet. "Pack your things. Just the essentials. Quick now."

"I need to let Junie out of the basement."

"In a minute."

"She's scared of the dark."

"We're all scared of something," he said, eyes wide and glittering.

"There's no proof against you."

"Sure there is. You got Meeker's bird cam. I'm sure it captured my car there in the lot that day."

"The bird camera didn't show your car," she blurted. "It showed Reggie Donaldson's. There's still no proof to convict you of a crime. We don't need to run away."

"Reggie was the guy Tucker was meeting?" He considered a moment, chuckling. "Imagine that. But it's all out now, and I've decided on a plan, so stop talking. Pack."

On shaking legs, she went to the bedroom, and he followed right behind her. She took out a bag and dumped in some clothes. All the while she wondered how she could escape, or at least leave a message so someone would know the truth about John Bender.

It made sense now. His constant presence in their lives, his utter devastation after LeeAnn's death, was driven by love, twisted into madness.

"That's enough. Let's go."

"I have to use the bathroom. Junie does, too."

"June will be fine. Can't you wait?"

She shook her head.

He smiled indulgently, like a devoted lover. He walked her to the bathroom and eyed the tiny window. "If you try to leave me," he said quietly, "I'll make sure you never see June again." Then he offered a bright smile. "We're going to be a family, remember?"

She shut herself in the bathroom, struggling to

quell the panic. He'd hurt Junie to make her comply. She couldn't escape. Quietly opening a drawer, she found a nearly used-up lipstick. In a corner of the mirror that wouldn't be visible from the door, she scrawled a message.

"John killed her."

"Time's up," John said. "Come out, come out, wherever you are."

Mick arrived at Keeley's house to find both Aunt Viv's car and Keeley's Jeep in the driveway. Aunt Viv waved at him from the porch step. He hoped she was not going to give him another hug until he noticed she wore a puzzled frown.

"Hello, Mick. Do you know where Keeley is?"

"Just left her an hour ago right here."

"Huh. Well, I can hear her cell phone ringing inside and she's not answering. Her car's here. Maybe she and Junie went for a walk."

Mick peered through the window. Mr. Moo Moo lay on the floor upside down, with his tail hanging over his eyes.

Mick went by Viv and pounded on the door. No answer. He tried the handle. Locked.

"I looked for the spare key, but it's not in the hiding place."

Dread trickled drop by icy drop through his spine. He went to Keeley's car, which had been left unlocked, and hit the garage door opener. He and Viv went into the house. There wasn't much out of place that he could see, except that some of her dresser drawers were open.

Viv emerged from the closet. "Her suitcase is gone."

The words hit him like blows. Had she decided to leave town? Not with the police still to be reckoned with, certainly not without Mr. Moo Moo. So what was the last thing she would have done before leaving with a small child? Insisted on that final potty break, he was sure, after hearing her discuss pertinent toilet training details with Viv. He still had no idea what training pants were, but he didn't need to know just then.

He went into the bathroom. Everything normal, no sign of distress.

Until his eyes fell on the tiny lipstick letters.

"Aunt Viv," he roared as he pounded out of the bathroom. "Get in the truck."

John carried a sobbing June to his car, parked a block away from the house.

"It's okay, Junie," she said. "Please let me hold her. She's scared."

"No," he said sharply. "You're driving and she's got to learn to respect her father." He thumped June on the back. "I would have been a stellar father. Did you know I was voted best marriage material in college? Respected profession, my own house, a healthy savings account. All that and you still picked that loser over me."

Keeley bit back a retort. "I'm sorry," she forced herself to say. "That's in the past. But we don't have to leave. We can stay here. Live in your house. We don't need to go to Mexico."

"Time for a fresh start. If Rivendale does happen to survive, I don't want him in our lives."

She got into the driver's seat, hoping he would put June next to her.

Instead he put her beside him in the back.

"She needs her car seat," Keeley tried desperately.

"Only a short drive. You'll be okay, won't you, June?"

June's face was wet with tears, and she shoved her fingers into her mouth.

"We forgot Mr. Moo Moo, her toy. Can I please get it?"

"Drive to my office. Now."

Maybe someone would see them at the office. She could get help. A spark of hope lit inside her until she checked her watch. It was five. Closing time. No clients would be milling around. Sweat dampened her forehead. There had to be some way to get June to safety.

They pulled up at the office and got out.

"Okay," he said. "This will only take a minute or two. I've got to get some cash out of the safe and grab the tickets and we're on our way." His smile was bright. He opened the trunk, and before Keeley knew what he was doing, he'd shoved June inside and slammed the lid.

"No," she screamed. "Let her out."

"Shh." He put a finger to his lips. "This won't take long, but if you raise a fuss—" He shrugged and put the keys in his pocket. "Come on."

Keeley fought for breath. Junie would be terrified in the trunk. "I won't go into the office until you let her out."

He frowned, eyes glittering. "That's not how you talk to your husband." He grabbed her by the arm. She thrashed and tried to break his hold, but his grip was like iron.

"The longer this takes, the stuffier it's going to get in that trunk." He unlocked the door and pushed her inside, bolting the door again behind him. Her nerves screamed. Had he made it up about Mexico? Was he intending to do things to her, to kill her? Then what would happen to Junie?

Was there enough air in that trunk?

Viv called Uttley, who was en route within moments.

"I'm already in town," Uttley snapped over the speakerphone. "I'll radio Dispatch. Stay in the parking lot," he commanded.

It didn't even register with Mick. Tires squealed as he peeled into the lot. He was charging up the door when he stopped so suddenly he almost fell.

"Did you hear that?"

Viv panted up behind him. "Yes, a thump, from John's car."

The trunk was locked, the doors, too, but he could see a release lever underneath the dashboard. He tore to his truck, popped the hood and ripped out the spark plug.

"What are you doing?" Viv wailed.

He had no time to explain the fastest way to break a window. A marine buddy of his who went to work for animal control showed him how, after he'd broken a window to save an overheated retriever.

He grabbed a hammer from the truck and smashed the plug, breaking off the bits of ceramic. With all his strength he flung the porcelain pieces against the driver's-side window. It shattered with a crash into a million bits of tempered glass. He reached in and popped the trunk.

Junie blinked, cheeks scarlet, nose running. "Hey, June," he said, trying to morph his features into something friendly looking. The poor tiny creature was scared enough already. "It's okay now."

He lifted her from the trunk, and she snuffled her wet face against his chest, the sobs shaking her whole body. Fury made him forget to breathe for a moment. Bender was responsible for scaring the child.

Viv cried out, and he handed June immediately into her arms.

"Take Junie away from here. Walk toward the main road and flag down help if Uttley doesn't find you first."

Viv clutched Junie, instinctively rocking her in that way that all women seemed to know. "Where are you going?"

"To get Keeley," he said, sprinting toward the office.

TWENTY-ONE

John reacted immediately when he heard the sound of glass breaking. He shoved Keeley into the bird-board-and-care room, locking the door from the outside.

"I'll be right back," he said, voice grim.

She whirled around, panic welling up in her throat. The windows were too high for escape. Pounding on the door accomplished nothing but bruising her palm. Her screams bounced back at her until she leaned against the door panting, the birds adding their frantic squawking and wing-flapping to the noise. She looked helplessly for something, anything, that she could use to protect herself. Footsteps again echoed in the corridor.

"Keeley," John shouted. "We're going. Now!"

She had only seconds before he'd unlock the door and shove her down the hall. Would he go back for Junie? The thought of Junie locked in the trunk gnawed at her. In a moment she had an idea, her one and only shot at creating a diversion that might let her escape to her daughter.

She plunged through the room, opening all the cages, to the kestrel, the hummingbird, the two recovering barn owls, the raucous crows. The birds might just save her and Junie. "Come on, birds. Fly away. You're free."

They did not come out, too terrified by the noise.

Despair balled her stomach into an impenetrable knot. There was the sound of a lock being turned.

With an ungainly lurch, a crow stepped to the edge of his cage and took flight. As if encouraged by their compatriot, the barn owls did the same, followed by the hummingbird and the kestrel. In moments, the room was alive with flapping wings and agitated cries.

John burst through the door, ducking as the kestrel sailed low to avoid the owls. Instinctively he threw up a hand and Keeley shot by him, into the hallway.

He recovered and chased after her. "You won't leave me, LeeAnn. I won't let you leave me for that loser," he shouted. He closed the ground between them until he was three yards behind, then three feet.

She could hear his enraged breathing.

"LeeAnn," he shouted again.

She sprinted for the front door, crashing into the panic bar, falling through, landing hard on her knees.

He reached for her hair, but he never made contact.

Mick Hudson hit him with a punch so hard it took him off his feet and sent him flying backward. Nose streaming with blood, John scrambled to his feet. "LeeAnn is mine. I'll never let her go." He launched himself at Mick again.

This time, Mick got him in the stomach. John doubled over, wheezing. Mick grabbed him by the collar and hauled him up until they were eye to eye. "That was for locking Junie in the trunk."

John shot him a look filled with hatred.

"And the woman's name is Keeley," Mick added, handing him over to Uttley.

Mick helped Keeley to her feet and smothered her in a hug. She clutched him close, shuddering in terror, unable to even feel the strong arms holding her close.

"Junie…" she gasped.

"She's okay. She's with your aunt in Uttley's car."

In a moment, Viv approached, carrying Junie. "She's here. Junie is here."

Keeley took her, crying and gulping in air at the same time. Junie cried, too, wrapping her chubby arms around Keeley's neck.

"Oh, Junie." How could she tell her? Dr. John Bender, the man they'd counted as a friend, had murdered LeeAnn. How close he'd come to destroying their family.

She found that her knees were wobbly, so Mick guided her to Uttley's car. "Here, sit down."

"The birds," she gasped.

"An officer has the room closed up again," Mick said. "They're calling a local vet to help get them in their cages." He smiled. "That was smart thinking, to create a diversion like that."

Junie lay down on the backseat and hid her face in her hands, a habit she had when life became too much for her. Keeley wished she could do the same.

"He killed my sister," she whispered, "and all this time I blamed Tucker."

Mick knelt down next to her until he could look into her eyes. "Don't hang on to that, Keeley. It's not what God wants, and it can cost you dearly." He put a big hand on her cheek and stroked it. "Trust me on that one."

He looked as though he wanted to say more, but the scene intensified as two more police cars pulled up, sirens wailing.

Junie moaned at the noise, and Keeley began to rub her back, just like she'd done when Junie was a newborn in the hospital.

"We're safe now, Junie Jo," she said. "We're finally safe."

When she again raised her head, Mick had moved away, telling his story to a cop and Chief Allen.

Their glances connected across the parking lot. Mick's shirt was rumpled, his knuckles dark with

John's blood or his own torn flesh. He nodded slightly, as if he'd somehow heard what she'd just said to June.

"You're safe now," she imagined him saying in that deep growl of his.

Finally.

A series of police officers approached the car, and the next time Keeley looked up, Mick was gone.

She did not make it to the hospital until the next day. Junie looked her best, fine hair contained in two pigtails, wearing her nicest red-checked dress and shiny patent-leather shoes. There was no way Keeley could convince June to take her fingers out of her mouth, but at least she was not crying. She'd finally fallen into an exhausted sleep in Keeley's lap on the rocking chair, and there they'd stayed all night.

Keeley did not mind her stiff back and the twinge in her neck. Junie was safe, once and for all. Now it was time to make things right.

After a deep breath, she tapped on the door and stepped into the hospital room.

Tucker straightened on the pillows and pushed the long hair out of his eyes. He was thin, chin stubbled with black, and there was an IV hooked up to his arm.

"How are you feeling?" she said.

He shrugged. "Okay. They say I might get released tomorrow, maybe."

The silence stretched long. Tucker's eyes roved over Junie, not with love, not yet, but curiosity and a touch of sadness.

"I know her name's Junie, but what's her middle name?"

Keeley stopped him, gently removing Junie's fingers from her mouth. "Tell Mr. Rivendale your name?"

"June Josephine Stevens," she fired off, promptly stuffing her fingers back into her mouth.

He smiled for a moment before it faded. "And she's got…" He trailed off, looking embarrassed.

"Junie has Down syndrome," Keeley said firmly. "She's got forty-seven chromosomes instead of forty-six. She's the same as every other three-year-old in most ways. It just takes her a bit longer to learn some things and her muscles don't do what she wants sometimes."

"Mine, either," Tucker said. "She's got LeeAnn's eyes."

"Yes," Keeley said, throat thick. "And she has your smile."

"You think so?"

Keeley nodded. "I do." She heaved in another deep breath. "Tucker, I'm very sorry about misjudging you."

He lifted a shoulder. "In some ways you were probably right. I was looking for the quick buck, which got me into trouble in the first place, gave Reggie an easy way to get to me even when I went clean. I deserved much of what I got. Told the same thing to Mick earlier."

"Mick was here?"

He nodded. "Couple of hours ago. On his way out of town."

Her heart plummeted. "Oh. Well, I'm glad you got to talk to him."

"Should have gone to him when Reggie started pressuring me, but I figured Mick was in on it. I guess I misjudged him, too."

"You didn't deserve to be blamed for LeeAnn's death, and I'm truly sorry. I'm sorry for not telling you that June was yours." She grasped Junie a little tighter. "You're her father and if…if you want to be a part of her life, that would be a good thing."

"LeeAnn knew I could be a jerk," he said, chewing his lip. "I'm sure that's why she didn't tell me. She knew I didn't want to be a dad. I'm not the greatest role model."

"You loved my sister. That's enough."

He broke into that wide, infectious grin that she sometimes saw on her daughter's face. "I'd like to visit sometime."

She returned the smile, which did not push back the sadness she felt knowing that Mick Hudson was gone. "We'd like that."

* * *

Mick walked in the hospital lobby, sat awkwardly in a chair too small for his long legs, paced around for a while and then went back outside. He tried strolling casually around the landscaped front where there was a walking path designed to calm visitors. Strolling was not a thing he'd ever mastered, and after he startled an older lady with a cane who looked at him as if he was going to mug her, he gave up and went back to the truck, leaning on the front bumper, hands in his pockets.

He saw Keeley come out, hair shining in the sunlight. Something warm and rich blossomed in his stomach as he watched her put Junie down and straighten the little girl's pigtails, which had gotten awry. The warm sensation was followed by cold prickles. Terror, to be precise. What was he doing? When had his life motto of caution and good sense flown right out the proverbial window?

The answer was easy. The moment he'd woken up on her couch, the second he'd seen her cock that chin in brilliant determination to protect her daughter.

The instant she'd thrown his check back at him with stubborn pride.

He swallowed, waved at them.

Keeley joined him, puzzled. "I thought you'd left."

"I did. Went to see my dad. Came back. How'd it go with Tucker?"

She sighed. "I think it's going to be okay. He wants to get to know June when he puts his life back in order."

"He's earned that right, I guess."

She nodded.

He stood, blowing out a breath. The words exited his mouth in a rush. "I came back to buy you a bread machine."

She blinked. "What?"

Had he really said that? "I wanted to get you one, a new one, before I left."

"Oh. Well. That was nice."

He fumbled on, like a clumsy bird at the edge of the nest. "And I was standing there in front of all the machines on the shelf, and I realized I like the one you have, because it's duct-taped, because you try to fix things yourself." He swallowed. "Like you fixed me," he added.

Junie squatted down in the grass bordering the parking lot, looking for bugs.

"Mick," Keeley said, brow furrowed, "what are you trying to say exactly?"

"I'm no good at it." He scrubbed a hand over his face "The words just don't come out right."

"Just say what's inside you."

He pulled a paper from his pocket. "I wrote it down."

Her lips curved. "You wrote down what you wanted to say to me?"

"Yeah." What kind of a man needed notes? His face went hot, his body skewered by intense uncertainty.

"Read it."

"Well, uh, the first part here says—" He tried to clear the boulder from his throat. "It says Reasons Why I Love Keeley Stevens."

Her eyes widened. "It does?"

"Yes, ma'am," he said, face burning. "It sure does."

Her mouth opened in an O of shock.

He pushed on. "Number one is, 'She is determined, fierce about love and all the things that matter. She is both strong and gentle at the same time.'"

He looked at his shoes. A poet, he was not.

"Keep going," she said, voice almost a whisper.

"'When I am with her, I feel like I'm where God meant me to be.'" His throat thickened, hands sweaty on the paper.

"What's number three?"

He smoothed the paper and gently folded it shut, focusing now on her perfect face. "Number three is that I love you and Junie. I've spent the past decade hiding away from everything and everyone, and no one made me want to change that except you."

"Mick…" she said.

"I figured you might not see things like I do, and if you want to send me packing, I will respect that. You've got a child to raise and you have to put her first. That's as it should be."

They both looked at Junie, oblivious as she combed through the grass.

Keeley shook her head slowly. "I haven't trusted anyone."

"Guess you got your reasons after what happened to LeeAnn."

"And now I've got even better reasons, since it turns out it was John who killed her." Tears shimmered in her eyes, and he caught the slight stiffening in her posture.

He felt a pain in his chest. She did not want him, didn't trust him; too much had happened in the past that would prevent them from having a future. He should walk away, except for the flood of love rising in his body that kept him rooted there. He could not leave, not until he knew for sure.

He pulled a ring from his pocket.

She stared at the gold circle.

"It was my mother's. She was an amazing woman, and I asked Dad if he would mind if it was worn by another amazing woman. He said it would be an honor." Mick dropped to one knee. "Would you marry me, Keeley?"

She gaped. "I…"

"I know I don't deserve you, but I promise every day of my life to try to make you happy."

A single tear trickled down her cheek, but still she did not speak.

"And I've got one more thing to say, but I didn't write this part down, either, so it's gonna come out rough." He rose and fished in his pocket with the other hand. He found the little gold bracelet with the gold heart charm and held it up, the sunlight burnishing it to brilliance. "This is for Junie. I'm not her father, and really you're all the parent she needs from what I can see, but if you allow me the honor of joining your family, I will do my best by her as long as I'm alive."

Then he knelt there again, with a ring in one hand and the bracelet in the other, looking into the vivid blue eyes of the most precious gift God had ever graced him with, knowing she might very well be about to turn him down.

Slowly, very slowly, she bent down, put one soft hand on his cheek and whispered, "I love you, too, Mick, and I want to spend the rest of my life with you."

Joy, freedom, grace and euphoria raced through his veins at the same time. He leaped to his feet, put the ring on her finger and pulled her in for a kiss.

Her soft mouth fit against his, so intimate and tender that it felt like a mingling of his soul with hers. He trailed his hands through her hair and she stroked the back of his neck. He did not think he had room inside for one more iota of joy.

Until Junie pulled at the leg of his jeans.

"Up, up," she said, arms outstretched and demanding.

Keeley laughed as he lifted and settled Junie onto his shoulders. She slid the sparkling bracelet onto

Junie's wrist. Junie examined it with awe. "You're going to have to stop doing everything she wants, you know."

"Oh," he said, jiggling Junie until she laughed. "I'll work on that. There's something I wondered about."

"What's that?"

"How old does she have to be before I can teach her how to change a spark plug?"

Keeley's chuckle was pure and sweet. "Maybe we should wait until she's got the hang of a few other things first."

"Fine by me," he said, leaning down and kissing Keeley again. "I've got all the time in the world."

* * * * *

Dear Reader,

I have a family of kites living in the tall pines near my yard. They are a type of raptor with snowy-white feathers and a strident squawk. They roost together in groups and defend their nests vigorously. Their most amazing behavior is their ability to hover while they search for prey. Imagine a pure white bird hovering with perfect skill and coordination, and you'll understand how they got their nickname of Angel Hawk. It makes me marvel at God's incredible engineering.

As the kites tend to their nests high overhead, I think of Keeley, the protagonist of this book. Dropped unexpectedly into the role of mother, she learns to trust herself to be the parent to a child with special needs. Coping with her own grief and fear, she must step away from the sheltering branches and trust that God will show her the way. Keeley finds help from an unlikely source. Mick is a man with no parenting skills, either, put into Keeley's path to become her life partner. Both will struggle before they learn that God is enough to equip them to meet the challenges that lie ahead.

It's so comforting to remind myself of that when the wind is buffeting me, and I feel as though I'm making no headway through stormy skies. I hope it is a comfort to you also, as you read this book. I am so appreciative of my readers for spending time with me and my books. If you have any thoughts or comments to share, you can reach me via my website at danamentink.com, or through Facebook. There is also a physical address on the website if you prefer to correspond by letter.

Thank you and God bless!
Dana Mentink

LARGER-PRINT BOOKS!

GET 2 FREE LARGER-PRINT NOVELS PLUS 2 FREE MYSTERY GIFTS

Love Inspired

Larger-print novels are now available...

LILPDIR13R

REQUEST YOUR FREE BOOKS!
2 FREE WHOLESOME ROMANCE NOVELS IN LARGER PRINT
PLUS 2
FREE
MYSTERY GIFTS

☀☀☀☀☀☀☀☀☀☀☀☀☀☀☀☀☀☀☀☀☀☀
HEARTWARMING™
☀☀☀☀☀☀☀☀☀☀☀☀☀☀☀☀☀☀☀☀☀☀
Wholesome, tender romances

YES! Please send me 2 FREE Harlequin® Heartwarming Larger-Print novels and my 2 FREE mystery gifts (gifts worth about $10). After receiving them, if I don't wish to receive any more books, I can return the shipping statement marked "cancel." If I don't cancel, I will receive 4 brand-new larger-print novels every month and be billed just $4.99 per book in the U.S. or $5.74 per book in Canada. That's a savings of at least 23% off the cover price. It's quite a bargain! Shipping and handling is just 50¢ per book in the U.S. and 75¢ per book in Canada.* I understand that accepting the 2 free books and gifts places me under no obligation to buy anything. I can always return a shipment and cancel at any time. Even if I never buy another book, the two free books and gifts are mine to keep forever.

161/361 IDN F47N

Name	(PLEASE PRINT)

Address	Apt. #

City	State/Prov.	Zip/Postal Code

Signature (if under 18, a parent or guardian must sign)

Mail to the Harlequin® Reader Service:
IN U.S.A.: P.O. Box 1867, Buffalo, NY 14240-1867
IN CANADA: P.O. Box 609, Fort Erie, Ontario L2A 5X3

* Terms and prices subject to change without notice. Prices do not include applicable taxes. Sales tax applicable in N.Y. Canadian residents will be charged applicable taxes. Offer not valid in Quebec. This offer is limited to one order per household. Not valid for current subscribers to Harlequin Heartwarming larger-print books. All orders subject to credit approval. Credit or debit balances in a customer's account(s) may be offset by any other outstanding balance owed by or to the customer. Please allow 4 to 6 weeks for delivery. Offer available while quantities last.

Your Privacy—The Harlequin® Reader Service is committed to protecting your privacy. Our Privacy Policy is available online at www.ReaderService.com or upon request from the Harlequin Reader Service.

We make a portion of our mailing list available to reputable third parties that offer products we believe may interest you. If you prefer that we not exchange your name with third parties, or if you wish to clarify or modify your communication preferences, please visit us at www.ReaderService.com/consumerchoice or write to us at Harlequin Reader Service Preference Service, P.O. Box 9062, Buffalo, NY 14269. Include your complete name and address.

HWDIR13R